W9-BTB-250

Nikolaj Frobenius is a Norwegian novelist and screen writer who has written many books and screenplays including that of the classic Nordic film thriller *Insomnia*, which was adapted into a major Hollywood production in 2002 starring Al Pacino and Robin Williams, and Dragonfly, which was released in 2001. In 2011 he adapted his own novel, the semi-autobiograhical *Teori og praksis* into the film *Sønner av Norge* (Sons of Norway).

Born in Oslo, he grew up at Rykkinn and studied film writing and research in London. His books have been acclaimed both in Norway and internationally, and have been translated into eighteen languages, including English, French, Spanish, Italian, German, Russian and Danish. He is a former editor of the periodical *Vinduet* and worked as a commissioning editor for Norsk filmfond from 2005–2008. He lives and writes in Oslo.

Frank Stewart spent most of his working life as a family doctor. He studied languages after he retired, and now works freelance as a translator. He gratefully acknowledges the co-operation of the author and the editing skills and helpful suggestions of his wife Margaret and daughter Ellie.

Also available in English

De Sade's Valet

DARK BRANCHES

Nik Frobenius

Translated by Frank Stewart

SANDSTONEPRESS
HIGHLAND | SCOTLAND

First published in Great Britain
and the United States of America
Sandstone Press Ltd
Dochcarty Road
Dingwall
Ross-shire
IV15 9UG
Scotland.

www.sandstonepress.com

Published in English in 2015 by Sandstone Press Ltd
English language editor: Robert Davidson

This translation has been published with the financial support of NORLA.
The publisher acknowledges subsidy from
Creative Scotland towards publication of this volume.

ISBN: 978-1-910124-53-6
ISBNe: 978-1-910124-54-3

Cover design by Brill
Typesetting by Iolaire Typesetting, Newtonmore
Printed and bound by Totem, Poland

April, 2012

1

'Good news, Joe! Your novel is back from the printers.'

Her eager tone startled me. Iben Hole didn't usually sound so enthusiastic over the phone. She wasn't the type to raise her voice. I would describe her as a whisperer, a person you have to lean forward to listen to, anxious not to miss the words slipping almost imperceptibly from her lips. Listening to her breathing I realised that, in my amazement, I hadn't answered. Not so much as a word to confirm that I was listening.

'Hello? Are you there?'

'Yes. Yes, I'm here.' Gazing out over the sea I realised that I was smiling. A cargo ship was sailing slowly across the horizon.

'The cover looks good,' she said, in her usual quiet tone. 'Shall I send you the proof copy, or do you want to come to our office to fetch it yourself?'

Iben had been my editor since my debut, six years earlier. Among my fellow authors she was known as 'The Falcon', because she was a sharp-eyed reader, critical and well-informed. Moreover, she could salvage texts that had hit the rocks.

'I'm in Stavern, at the hut,' I said, looking down towards the shore where my daughter, Emma, was playing with a friend, a little local girl with round glasses. 'Can you send it to me?'

The early April sunshine was strong and tempting. Easter was over, but we planned to stay for a couple of days longer. Agnes, my partner, didn't have to be back in town before the next week. It was meant to be a long holiday, but I already felt the urge to get back, settle down with the book, go through it page by page, check the page numbering and typography, see it on paper, scrutinise the cover.

I held my hand up to my eyes. The girls had found an old oar among the stones and were dragging it through the grass towards the gravel road. Dark and slippery, it looked as if it was smeared with oil. When they lost their grip and let it drop between them, I wondered what the devil they were going to do with the damned thing.

Emma started calling: 'Daddy!'

'I'll set off by car early tomorrow,' I said to Iben, taking a few paces towards the jetty, 'and ring you when I get home'.

'Fine. Give me a call as soon as you've looked at it. By the way, did you see the trailer on TV?'

'The trailer ... ?'

'About the book programme ...'

'Ah ... No I didn't.'

The channel had made an advertising clip for the culture programme where I was to be interviewed.

'Was it OK?'

'It was ...'

The sentence was broken off by a nasty squealing on the telephone line.

'Iben?'

There was just a hissing in the phone, and I suddenly imagined that Iben had been struck by some sort of phonic lameness where the vocal cords were unable to produce whole words, only incomprehensible guttural sounds.

'... mo ... forb ... ann ...mfrg ...'

'Iben. Are you there?'

4

The connection broke off completely. I replaced the phone and went down towards the two little girls and the greasy oar.

I had written an autobiographical novel from my childhood, a dark and disturbing chapter in the story of my life, and never before had a work of mine attracted so much attention, never before had the people in the publishing house been so engaged and enthusiastic.

You've cracked it now, was what most of them said. I took this to mean that they reckoned my writing would at last reach a bigger audience. *That* didn't mean so much to me. How many people read the book was not the most important thing. What I most cared about was that those who did read it considered it authentic.

The novel described people and events in my own life, and I had never before dared to write anything so personal and real and true. I reckoned it was a breakthrough for me as an author. I had worked extra hard to depict as accurately as possible what had happened, opening up old wounds, and delving into matters which previously I had wanted to forget. Maybe readers would realise that I had gone out of my comfort zone to capture the disturbing events fully.

It was late Easter and spring had already come to Stavern. We ate lunch on the terrace.

The hut belonged to Agnes's father. It was a functional building from the 1970's, discreetly redecorated a few years ago; nothing fancy, but clean-styled and effective. Her dad was retired, and lived here most of the year, but was presently travelling with a former colleague from the architectural studio. They were visiting some restored old vineyards in Southern France, which sounded to me like an excuse to get drunk every day for a month. 'Just borrow the hut while I'm away,' he had said, and Agnes had jumped at the chance.

5

Her father was a stylish, sombre, taciturn man and, when I thought about it, I realised that I knew next to nothing about him. Agnes seldom spoke about him. He had brought up his daughter on his own, Agnes's mother having died of a stroke shortly after the birth, but I had no impression it bothered him. He always seemed remarkably content, one of those men who are fully satisfied with their own company and, strictly speaking, don't need the company of other people. With the exception of Agnes, he showed a conspicuous and nonchalant indifference about others. With her he exchanged rapid glances and comments which nobody else understood. It was as if father and daughter had their own intimate and indecipherable language.

Agnes had little outward resemblance to her father. Fair, her delicate face and skin were so pale that many people thought she was sick. She was the quietest girl in the class, never raising her voice, and didn't put her hand up unless it was really necessary. She was the girl in the back row whom nobody particularly bothered about when she was there, and whose absence hardly anyone noticed when she wasn't.

I had realised pretty quickly that there were two sides to Agnes.

The quiet, kind, unassuming girl.

And the calculating, complicated, ruthless competitor.

She was undoubtedly the most ambitious in our class. She hid behind tough Katinka, but I realised that it was Agnes who was in control, whispering to her friend what to do. Agnes didn't like to stand out, but she did want to be Number One. She wanted to get into the best schools, to become a lawyer and earn millions and live in a luxury villa with a swimming pool. She would have a big and incredibly successful family, and her eyes shone when she spoke about it.

These were childhood dreams, and now that she was an adult she laughed at what she had been like. 'So shamelessly ambitious,' she said. 'Good God, I don't know where that

6

came from. Nobody in my family is like that at all. And I'm not really like that either!'

Nobody who knew her was taken in. Her image and her ideals had softened, but we all knew that a calculating little monster still sat in her head, studying and evaluating situations, on the look-out for opportunities.

I didn't think that she was duplicitous or deceitful, rather that she had two sides which took it in turn to dominate: an incredibly kind, self-effacing side, and a ruthless strategist. Sometimes I got the feeling that I was partner to two people in one and the same woman, but I had learned to like both, or perhaps their combination. If she had been only the very kind, unassuming Agnes, living with her would eventually have become unbearable.

I poured more tea for her.

'I'm going back to town tomorrow. The proof copy of my novel has arrived. I want to go through it carefully.'

She nodded. 'Just go.'

'Are you cross?'

She threw up her hands. 'Cross? Good God, yes, of course! Just go.'

She knew how important it was for me to check that everything was in order with the book. An error could have crept in. Once we had sent a whole first edition for shredding because of a serious error in the typesetting.

I stirred a spoonful of honey into the tea, watching how it floated, broke up and dissolved.

'We'll be fine.'

Emma came running down the path with a dark gash on her arm. Only when I got up did I see that she was laughing.

Agnes looked up at me with a surprised smile.

'Did you think there had been an accident?'

'I don't know …' I called to Emma: 'What's that on your arm?'

Emma came to a stop under the terrace. Looking herself

over in surprise, she loosened a band of black seaweed from her forearm and threw it onto the terrace.

'It's only seaweed!'

The seaweed hit my shirt. I plucked off the clingy clump, swung it round my head and threw it back. She dodged gleefully into hiding.

Emma was six, due to start school in the autumn. After she had gone to bed, I found the trailer for the book programme on the internet. Agnes slid down beside me on the sofa.

She often made unsympathetic comments on culture programmes, which she thought were self-important and meaningless. I was nervous when I had to show her a programme I was taking part in.

The trailer only lasted thirty seconds. It showed the faces of myself and the programme leader, Siri Greaker, and the cover of the book.

Agnes said: 'It looks good!'

She grasped my hand and I felt her warm fingers on my forearm. Tingling with excitement, I leant forward to kiss her. She smelled of woods and moss.

'I'd forgotten that you were doing this.' She stroked her fingers back and fro across my arm. 'Maybe this'll be your breakthrough,' she said, affectionately.

Agnes had trained as a lawyer but made a surprising career change several years before; she quit the legal firm where an illustrious career was predicted and took a more poorly paid job in a humanitarian organisation providing aid for asylum seekers. She told me: 'I'm a competitive type, but suddenly I couldn't manage to compete anymore.'

I closed my eyes and laid my head in her lap for a few moments while she stroked my hair. I had a vision of a dying elephant and a girl stroking the big, sad creature's trunk.

The next day, I drove too fast on my way to Oslo. Around Liertoppen I thought that there was a police car on my tail, but it was only an ambulance. I turned the radio on, the classic music programme, and Mozart's piano concerto number 21 flooded from the speakers, my mother's favourite piece. I slowed down.

As I drove up Maridalsveien grey weather drifted in. Our crooked house was at the end of Frysjaveien, in the middle of a little group of old wooden houses. New blocks of flats had gradually grown in a circle around it, terraced houses, commercial buildings and underground garages.

When my father bought the house in 1973, this was mainly a working class area. He was part of the new age, the new middle class. The funeral directors Uddermann & Son undeniably displayed the sober gravity which characterised undertakers of that era, but had not yet adopted the service-orientated smoothness of the new age. Sometimes I thought it was only a matter of time before our old house would be bought and torn down and the site developed into something more imposing and valuable.

I parked the car in the garage and went straight to the letterbox, sorting the post as I unlocked the door and switched on the light in the kitchen. No package with a book and no note from the post office, only a handful of bills, two copies of the local paper and a letter without the name of the sender. My name and address were scribbled aslant across the front of the envelope in unsteady handwriting, as if it had been written with the wrong hand: *Author Joe Uddermann*. I opened it at the kitchen table, using a kitchen knife.

Inside was a press cutting from the local paper, *Nordre Aker Budstikke* of 23rd October 1990. There was a black and white picture of the old Grefsen school, with the headline: 'School fire extinguished.'

I turned the envelope over several times and shook it. It didn't contain any greeting.

9

Had someone at the publishers sent it as a joke?

I called Iben. 'No book,' I said.

'Strange.'

'Instead I got a letter, with an old press cutting about the fire at the school.'

'Oh?'

'It's surely not somebody with the publisher who has sent me this?'

'What? No, I don't think so. It must be someone who has seen the trailer.'

The trailer. Obviously.

'You'll surely get the book tomorrow, Joe.'

I hung up and looked at the cutting again. There was a drawing at the bottom of the page, a little skull. So bloody childish, I thought, folding it up.

Later, as I lay on the sofa watching the news, I couldn't get the macabre embellishment out of my thoughts. Who draws a skull, puts it in an envelope and sends it to an author? I wanted to call Agnes, but it was already eleven o'clock and she and Emma had probably gone to bed.

When the late evening news was over I went downstairs to my office and switched on the computer. After replying to some e-mails I tidied my desk and looked at all the files in the folder labelled *The Chalk*.

Agnes said that I was impossible to live with in the weeks leading up to the completion of the novel. I flew off the handle over trivia and was remote and distracted. There were days when I was so gloomy I couldn't speak to anyone.

I had already published three novels, but the fourth was no easier. Bringing a book to completion is like taking a child out into the back yard and shooting it, wrote Truman Capote. I had stuck the quotation on the wall as a reminder that I was not the only person who felt that completing a novel is a crime. Shutting down the computer I switched off the light and went up to the kitchen, where I drank a glass of

10

wine and swallowed a sleeping pill. After eight hours I awoke with a dry taste in my mouth. I couldn't remember what I had dreamed about, but had a feeling that it was something important.

After breakfast I sat in the garden with a cup of coffee and an old crime novel by the legendary American author David Goodis. The cover showed the young author behind a writing desk, looking up with a resolute and determined expression. I had always thought that I ought to read his work, but had never got round to it, and wondered whether this may have been because it was not so much the crime novels I was interested in, as the author's own story; his 'inner demons and increasing alcoholism,' his preference for 'brutal women', his 'shabby overcoat', his concern for his mentally retarded brother.

Goodis as an author was a classic tragedy, obviously talented but chronically unlucky. He lacked self-confidence and was exploited by cynical film producers. True to the tragic theme, he ended his days in the mud, probably beaten to death in a back street where he was looking for a moment of bliss.

To me, he represented the prototype of the 21st century author; a self-imposed outcast with asocial personality traits, useless in the mass media technological society except as a person the producers of fiction could steal stories from.

Clouds descended on the hillside and the riverbed below our house, when I had only reached page eleven in the story of innocent, doomed Vince Perry.

I saw in my mind's eye the title of my own book, the font they had used and the photograph of a fair-haired little boy gazing down at the fire he had started. Would this book too end up on the scrapheap of oblivion, in the missed opportunities department? Or would it be my breakthrough – to what?

At eleven o'clock I went to the post-box, even though the post was not usually delivered until later. There was a padded C5 envelope in the box.

When I picked it up, I saw that it had been opened. Looking up and down the road I saw no sign of the post van or of anybody else, but I nevertheless had a feeling that someone was watching.

At the kitchen table I inspected the book cover. Nothing wrong, all as planned. I began to go through the book page by page, to check whether any errors had crept into the text at the printers.

Everything seemed fine, so I sent a text message to Iben: *All in order*.

Then I picked up the envelope again. Turned it over and over. First the anonymous letter. Now this. Was it a coincidence?

Iben replied to my text and reminded me of the TV interview I was to give a few days later.

In the dusk I went jogging along the narrow path which goes down to the river bank. When I came to Oset, I paused to watch wisps of mist floating over Lake Maridal. The buildings of the water purification plant lay on the hillside like a secluded military camp. Swallows were circling over the surface of the water and I thought of the girl I had once kissed at a group of huts deep in the woods, remembering the feel of her smooth, penetrating tongue.

Arriving back home, I saw the shape of my neighbour's back on his enormous, newly built terrace. He was bent over, talking into his mobile in what I thought was a secretive, self-righteous, enthusiastic tone. This worried me. What on earth was he planning now? I took a little stone from the gravel path and pressed it hard into the palm of my hand. The short, sharp pain felt liberating.

I stood under the shower for so long that my scalp felt as if it would split.

While I was sitting at the kitchen table afterwards, wondering why the envelope containing my novel had been

12

opened, Agnes called to ask if I had forgotten to pay the telephone bill. We had a NetCom family subscription in my name. There was something wrong with the mobile phone, she said.

'The bill is paid,' I replied, shuffling through the mail.

'Are you sure?'

I opened the envelope from NetCom. The bill was for 1456 kroner.

'What do you really think of me?' I asked. I reckoned I could pay the bill right away by internet banking.

'You're a smart one,' she replied, but it didn't sound as carefree as she perhaps thought. Lately I had had a nagging feeling that she no longer trusted me.

'How's Emma?

'Emma's fine.'

'Where is she now?'

'She's sitting right here.'

'Can I speak to her?'

I stood up and looked out into the garden. The two old apple trees were disappearing into the mist which was probably not going to clear.

'Hello Daddy,' said Emma distractedly.

'Are you watching TV?'

'No.'

'What have you been doing today?'

'Rebekka and I played by the shore.'

'Alone?'

'Yes.'

'I hope you didn't go out on the ruined pier'?

'No, but we found a man lying asleep in Granddad's boat.'

'What?'

'Mum said he was a tramp, but he didn't look like that. He had chewing gum.'

'Can I talk to her?'

Agnes reassured me. 'Don't worry. He was just a tramp.'

13

'*A tramp?* A gipsy?'

'They're called Romanies, not gipsies. But I don't know. I didn't see him.'

'Emma says he didn't look like a tramp.'

'Perhaps it's just something they have imagined. You know what youngsters are like. They chatter away and don't know the difference between truth and lies.'

'Don't they?' Did she really think that Emma was lying?

The phone went quiet.

'Are you alone?' she asked.

'Why do you ask? Of course I'm alone.'

'I can hear voices in the background.'

'It's just the radio. I'm missing you.'

'You just say that. Has the book arrived?'

'Yes. It looks OK.'

'Good.'

'Mm.'

'See you tomorrow.'

'Yes. I've got to give an interview, but I'll be back about two.'

'See you then.' She hung up.

We had been together for nineteen years and had known each other since primary school. I pictured her face in front of the big window which looked out over the bay and Stavernsodden Lighthouse. Her eyelids were pinched together and there was something she was upset about, something she hadn't been able to say.

I slept with my knees drawn up to my chest and dreamt that I was being chased round and round the kitchen by a wild boar and couldn't find a way out.

When I wakened at six, the mist was still clinging to the roofs, the trees, the veranda. Through the window I could hear the rustle of the Aker River, subdued and eerie.

I generally said that I lived in Frysja, even though that

14

wasn't really a proper place name and was a source of confusion. If anyone says 'Let's meet at Frysja,' it's really impossible to know where that is.

Originally Frysja was the name of the river which ran from Lake Maridal, and there are many little places along the river, between Lake Nydal and Lake Maridal, which are referred to as Frysja. The residential and industrial zone west of the Aker River was called Brekke. I ought to have said that I lived in Brekke, but I have always liked the name Frysja, even though nobody knows what it means; spume or foam in a river, perhaps.

As the fridge was almost empty I went shopping at the local supermarket, pushing the trolley between the shelves. A man in a brown leather jacket walked up to me, gripped the trolley and stopped. I looked at his sharp features in amazement. A man who has worked a lot out of doors, I thought, a forthright, handy guy with bloodshot eyes. His hair had once been light blond, but age had given it an indeterminate colour between grey and sand. His look nailed me.

'What the devil, you're hellish far away, Joe'

'Pardon?'

'Don't you recognise an old schoolmate?'

'Vebjorn?'

He had changed, grown from a timid little boy to a hulk with a scarred face. Vebjorn had had problems in Inner Telemark. He and Katinka had bought a little croft there in 2001 after they tired of Oslo, of partying with the same gang which steadily dwindled as family life and career commitments gradually killed the partying spirit. Family life was nothing to them, and apparently they were unable to have children, so they moved to the country to take up organic farming. Katinka had trained as a gardener, but a few years later I heard that it wasn't carrots they were growing.

Vebjorn bought high intensity lamps and fans for a growing

15

enterprise in the cellar, and Katinka's horticultural skills ensured good crops. He sold the produce by the kilogram to a middleman in Bjolsen and the cannabis factory flourished until he was caught and taken for a long 'holiday' in Horten Prison.

I smiled, but Vebjorn didn't seem to think it was strange to have met me. 'God, it's been a long time.'

'So have you moved back to your house in town?'

Business was still going well for Vebjorn. He and Katinka had bought a terraced house on the corner of Kjelsas Street and Lytter Street as an investment for the future. After renting for several years their tenants had been given notice and they were about to move in.

'Are you busy doing the place up, Vebjorn?'

'Maybe.' He peered away from me, no longer interested in small talk.Had he found out something? Had Katinka told him something about me?

The face in front of me was disturbingly serious. That twisted smile was long since gone, I thought, perhaps left in the cell at Horten. If Vebjorn and Katinka had been living in town we might have seen them from time to time as she had been Agnes's best friend. Life hadn't worked out like that, and now the man in front of me was a stranger.

'I heard that you had been speaking with Katinka,' he said, shoving my trolley backwards, pushing me up against the shelves with the handle pressing on my diaphragm.

'It was just for research, Vebjorn.'

'*Research*?' His voice was thick with anger. 'Keep away from her.' He jolted the trolley so hard that I stumbled backwards, fell against the shelf, banged my knee and got covered in packets of pasta spirals. His face was right over me, pale with rage.

'*Bloody author*!'

He went towards the checkouts and I had no chance to explain myself. Couldn't say anything. All I could see of Vebjorn now was hunched, threatening shoulders.

A young shop-girl helped me up, glancing nervously round about.

'Some people are mad,' I mumbled.

She wanted to know if I was alright, and if she should call the police.

'No, no, it's OK.' I said. 'That was just some poor idiot.'

Due at the TV studio at 08.30, I dragged myself out of bed with a sore knee, feeling like an old man who had been beaten up. There was a shabby mongrel in the garden, sniffing around. I tapped on the window with a fingernail and the skinny beast startled and bounded away into the mist.

I went through to the kitchen. It was already quarter past eight and I was late. I backed the car out of the garage, taking care not to bump into anything unseen in the mist. Turning on the radio produced only a hissing noise.

At the end of the Tasen tunnel the mist came down over the car. I heard the sound of a big lorry beside me but didn't see the front of the trailer until it was close against the side window.

I shouted at my windscreen: 'Watch where you're going, you idiot!'

As I swung into the car park at Marienlyst, I got my first sight of the windows of TV House through a gap in the mist. The car made a nasty scraping sound as I parked it, and I approached TV House with my heart thumping.

2

Driving back to Frysja, I had a feeling that Siri Greaker had tricked me into saying something I didn't want to say.

I didn't know where the slip of the tongue was, but was sure that a mistake had crept in and that when I saw the programme I would be ashamed and embarrassed. It was to be broadcast a week later. I couldn't work out where I could have gone wrong, so just tried to put it out of my thoughts. There were still two weeks before the book was due to be launched.

I swung through the gate and parked in front of our house. Emma was sitting on the steps looking through a picture book with Agnes, her Barbie doll lying in the pale grass. The mist had lifted and the sun was breaking through the clouds over Grefsen Hill.

I forgot about the TV interview and felt much more relaxed. Now I would concentrate fully on the family and try to be a little more 'with it'. I stuck my head out of the car window and called: 'Goldilocks!'

They looked up. They looked so fine together.

Emma stood up and folded her arms across her chest. 'My name isn't Goldilocks!'

'What is it then?'

'Emma!' she yelled, running towards me.

'Have you had a good time?'

She nodded, but showed me a little head she was holding in her hands. 'See what happened to Nora.'

I gently took the Barbie doll's head from her. It looked as

if her neck had been severed with a pair of scissors. 'Ugh. How did that happen?'

'Somebody cut her head off.'

'What?'

'The dolls were lying out on the step of the hut one night,' Agnes began.

'And when I lifted Nora up,' continued Emma,' I saw that her head had been cut off.'

'That's really sick,' I said.

'I think it was the boy from next door,' said Emma. 'The one who's daft in the head.' Her eyes darkened.

I stroked her hair, and felt a lump in my throat.

'Do you think we can stick it on again?'

I examined the doll's head more closely. 'Do you have the rest of the body?'

She nodded.

'We've got superglue,' I said. 'That sticks anything.'

She ran into the house.

On the step beside Agnes there was a half-eaten apple, already going brown. I bent forward to kiss her. Her lips were cool. I lay on top of her.

'How did the interview go?' she whispered.

I pushed her down onto the step, my hand crushing the half apple. Now I was lying over her, feeling the warmth from her belly and her breasts. I stroked her cheek and neck and kissed her again. 'It went fine.' I kissed her ear, stuck my hand in under her skirt and stroked her belly.

'Tell me then,' she laughed, punching my stomach. 'What did they ask about?'

I sat up. 'Everything.'

'So, are you going to be a celebrity now?'

I just smiled. 'Haven't you missed me?'

'No,' she replied, stroking my hair.

I loved her fingers. These long, cool fingers. They were the most fantastic and exciting thing about her. They enchanted me. I kissed them.

'Who is it that's *daft in the head*?'

'The boy from the farm.'

Her blonde forelock hung down over her eyes. She looked a little tired, with bags under her eyes, and I thought of her asleep, her lips opening and closing and her mouth making tiny movements and sounds.

She put her hand on my thigh. I looked down at her fingers. Her nail varnish was half scraped off.

'Let's fuck,' she whispered. Her hand slid right up to my prick. She bent forward and pressed her mouth against mine. She smelled of apple.

'What about Emma? Shouldn't I mend that doll's head?'

'You can do that later.' She kissed me.

We locked the bedroom door and undressed quickly. Agnes lay down. I kissed her thighs and squinted up towards her head which was turned sideways. She shut her eyes and mumbled. 'What are you waiting for?'

I worked my fingers slowly back and forwards in the moist, smooth cleft. It was like feeling moisture inside a stone. I went half-way into her.

She whimpered. 'Put it right in.'

Glad to be over with that damned interview I lunged right into her.

I had a muddled dream that night, something to do with an extra mouth which I had grown behind my first mouth and which burst into the TV interview.

'I'd so like to strangle you,' I said with a smile to Siri Greaker, the interviewer.

'Pardon?'

'You've got such a pretty neck.'

'What?'

20

'I'm sorry ... excuse me ...' I grasped her hands and kissed them. 'I don't know what came over me.'

'Let me go,' she whispered, but I didn't let her hands go. I held them tightly and kissed them and began to cry.

'I'm sorry, I'm sorry,' I whispered in a loathsome childish whispering tone. 'Can't you just pretend that I'm not here?'

3

I felt a surge of pride one day in early May when I saw my book on display in a bookshop at the big *Storo* shopping centre in Oslo.

The first reviews were positive, with one critic reporting that the novel had made a big impact on her. I knew her only by name, but I thought about her and imagined how the *big impact* might have made her blush. Several reviewers emphasised the novel's authenticity, and one praised my convincing description of the background of antisocial violence.

I spent several hours lying in the garden staring at the sky and feeling relieved, as if a boil had been lanced. I had a liberating sense of fatigue.

What had I been so worried about? Reviewers? The verdict of the readers? Or the fact that the novel was based on real events? Perhaps it had not been any of the written episodes, I thought, but a fear that something else had slipped into the text, something hideous which ought to have remained unthought and unwritten.

Now the worries were gone, and that night I slept dreamlessly. In the morning I awakened refreshed and like new, but when evening came I got round to thinking about the little skull which the anonymous sender had drawn on the old newspaper cutting and sent to me. That little drawing plagued me like an itch inside my head.

In the Chief Editor's office I met Iben and others from the publishing company to watch the TV programme. She and her colleagues seemed very pleased, but I didn't dare look at my own face or at the blunder I might have made. So I shifted my gaze to a photograph on the wall and focussed on an Egyptian pyramid.

Sparkling wine was served in plastic wine glasses. I heard my voice streaming out of the TV and marvelled at how a voice can change when it goes through a speaker.

'This is great,' said the Chief Editor. 'I think this book will sell well.'

My mouth was dry. 'Really?' None of my other books had sold particularly well.

'Yes, there's a special excitement, an unease in this text. I think many readers will be interested to find out what sort of people are capable of committing such acts.'

Everyone nodded and smiled. I did too, and high fived the Chief Editor whose hand was big and moist.

I don't know why I find it difficult to accept praise, but when anyone says something complimentary it arouses feelings of suspicion and I look for dubious motives.

Iben looked so happy. She didn't often look happy. There was a seriousness about her which I didn't think could be dispelled, but now she was bright and relaxed. I took away a DVD of the interview on which she had written with a felt pen: CONGRATULATIONS.'

When I got home, Agnes was sitting alone in the dark in the living room.

'You're sitting there in the dark?' She glanced up at me with dull eyes. 'Was it OK?'

'What?'

'The interview.'

'I didn't manage to see it all,' she said in a low voice. 'Someone rang in the middle.'

'Who?'

'Emma watched alone. She followed it very well in fact.' Agnes stroked her forelock away from her eyes.

'So you didn't get to see it?'

23

She shook her head.

I sat down beside her on the dark sofa. 'Is there something wrong?'

She gave me a long look. 'What do you mean?'

'You don't look right.'

She looked at me for a long time, saying nothing.

'What's the matter?'

She began to cry, deeply unhappy.

'Agnes,' I whispered, stroking her hair. 'Who was it that rang?'

'It was …' Her voice stuttered.

I hugged her close. 'Who?'

'I don't know … a voice … a man …'

A man. 'What did he say?'

She shook her head. 'It was horrible, Joe, the way he spoke.'

'What was it then?'

She mumbled something, raised her head and looked at me. 'That you were with a whore.'

'What?' I stared at her mouth.

She swallowed. He said: '*Your man is with a whore.*'

It felt as if she was sticking a fork right into my face. 'What the hell …'

Agnes closed her eyes and dried her tears with her hands. I wanted to comfort her, embrace her, but my hands felt numb and dead.

'Oh, my God, it's just some psychopathic nutcase,' I said. 'Some people stalk folk as soon as they appear on TV.

She looked up at me. 'But what does it mean? What he said? Did he mean me? That you are with me and that I am a whore, or that you have been with someone else, or what?'

'Don't think about it,' I said, as calmly as I could. It's just babble, just some damned psychobabble.

She nodded, but I could see she was still worried.

4

I wakened and stared at the ceiling. It was dark in the bedroom. Through a chink in the curtains I could see the dark shape of the apple trees stooping over the wall. No sound from anywhere. No cars, no running river. It seemed that the room was becoming smaller and lower and the ceiling was looming above my eyes. Agnes was lying very still and for a few seconds I panicked, until her eyelids twitched.

I got up and put on my dressing gown. In the pocket was a little hairbrush, which was Emma's. Two long, blonde strands of hair fell from it and settled on the floor like two white tracks. I put it back.

'Are you asleep?' I whispered, bending down over Agnes.

She didn't answer. I kissed her cheek carefully. She turned over in her sleep and pulled the duvet over her head.

Standing by the window, I gazed out into the garden, not wanting to think about the phone call, the man's voice, what he had said to Agnes: *Whore.*

I had grown up in this house. What had been my bedroom as a boy was now Emma's room. The garden hadn't changed much. When we took over we made many changes inside, but almost none outside. I wanted it to stay as it had always been. I liked the sloping lawn and the old apple trees, even though their roots were decaying and they really ought to be cut down.

Early sunlight fell obliquely onto the two old trunks. On lazy summer days my mother and father and my cousin and I used to lie in the garden with books and games and plastic cups with fizzy red juice.

Your man is with a whore.
Who the devil would call her to say such a thing?

Shutting my eyes I visualised Katinka's face, her mouth, her lips, the little cleft between her front teeth. When she closed her eyes and leant towards me I bent forward and kissed her. It could have been Vebjorn who had rung Agnes with the whore message. But Agnes would have recognised his voice, wouldn't she? Could Vebjorn have got someone else to call?

Would he do such a thing?

A thin, piping noise right behind me. I turned quickly.

'What are you looking at, Daddy?' Emma stood in the middle of the floor, hugging her Barbie doll. Was it Emma or the Barbie that made the sound? I looked at the doll in her hands. The lifeless face. Do Barbie dolls make noises?

'I'm looking at the apple trees,' I said, handing her the hairbrush. 'You've got such lovely hair.'

She took the hairbrush. 'Why are you looking at the trees?'

'I'm wondering whether they need to be cut down.'

'Oh, no! We can't do that.'

'Maybe we'll have to.'

'Why?'

'I'm afraid they're dying, my dear. How's Nora?'

She showed me the doll. I had carefully stuck the head back on, but now it was hanging to one side. The glue was beginning to crack. 'Oh dear.'

Emma looked anxiously down at the doll. 'She doesn't look good.'

I held the doll under the light on the kitchen bench and squeezed the whole contents of a tube of superglue into the narrow crack between head and neck.

'There. I think that will be better now,'

Emma looked at me doubtfully. 'I don't know,' she said disdainfully. 'I'm not sure she'll be right again.'

26

'I think she'll be fine, if we just let her rest. The glue needs to dry properly.'

She looked at the doll as if it had caught some horrible infectious disease. 'I don't think she'll make it. Her head's sure to fall off again. She's not as strong as my other dolls, and she's ugly.'

'No,' I tried to reassure her. 'I'm sure she'll be OK again.'

She inspected the scar which ran right across the doll's neck. 'She's so ugly, very ugly. I don't think I want her any more.'

I put my hand reassuringly on her shoulder. 'Lay her down so that she can rest a little, then we'll see. Perhaps she'll look a bit healthier by the evening.'

'OK then,' she said, and shuffled back into her room.

All day I thought about how good it would be to go jogging through the woods. After supper, when I had put on my tracksuit and jogging shoes, I found Emma standing behind me again in her pyjamas. Agnes was sitting on the rocking chair in the living room, reading a book with a familiar cover.

'Are you going running again?' asked Emma.

I smiled. 'Yes, and it's your bed-time.'

She watched me from the window with a solemn face, but didn't wave.

There was a dead squirrel lying in front of the garage door, one side of its head crushed, caught under the wheel of the neighbour's car. I found an old newspaper, carried the dead animal away and threw it in the rubbish bin. Then I stood for a few seconds, wondering whether I had done the right thing.

After parking the car at Sandermosen Station I ran up through the dark woods on the hillside, towards Sinober. There were very few people in the woods, and the air was cool. I enjoyed running in the evening. The spruce trees stood densely together on either side of the narrow track and I could feel the soles of my shoes sliding on their slippery roots

27

which stretched out over the path. After ten minutes I came to a group of huts and slowed down. Peering between the spruces I saw a woman sitting on the step in front of the old timber hut. Her dark hair cascaded over her shoulder and hid her face. She blew a pillar of cigarette smoke in front of her. I stopped sharp and felt the blood vessels in my neck pulsing.

I had been in contact with her while I was working on the book, because there were things I wanted to ask her. She had been interested in the person who started the fire, but how much had they really had to do with each other? I had phoned her at the end of August and invited her to meet me over coffee.

At high school I had been wildly in love with Katinka, but fortunately realised quite quickly that she was far too beautiful and stylish for me. Agnes and Katinka had been best friends, but Katinka was somebody Agnes had put behind her and I don't think they had seen each other more than a couple of times in the past ten years.

Her voice over the phone had taken me by surprise, as if a voice from my youth was pushing into my ear, and I had the dizzy and slightly unhappy feeling of being helplessly in love with a girl I could never have.

When we met a few days later in a coffee bar in Grefsen Street I was totally unprepared for how overcome I would be. The visual impact of Katinka's face in the lamplight aroused the same intense and chaotic feelings of frustration and longing and romantic affection that I felt at the age of thirteen. I must have been blushing when I sat on the sofa in front of her, because she laughed.

She looked wonderful, with her glowing skin and shiny hair. I couldn't conceal my feelings. I devoured her with my eyes and couldn't stop thinking what it would be like to kiss her, to undress her, to make love with this person who was, at the same time, an apparition from the days of our youth and an extremely attractive and very real thirty three year old woman. We chatted for more than an hour about what she was doing (working in a garden centre) and what I was doing (writing). Then we talked a little about our schooldays and I put my questions to her, while all the time watching her with a longing which really surprised me.

A week later I rang her and said I needed to ask a few follow-up questions. She hesitated for a moment before inviting me to the hut. We had seen each other five or six times over the past few months. Perhaps it was because we both knew there could never be any long term relationship that every meeting was filled with an almost frightening tension which at last, step by step, drew our bodies closer and closer together.

'Hi,' I said, walking over the clearing towards her.

Katinka looked at me from the step. The light from a paraffin lamp was flickering in the bedroom window. The smoke from her cigarette spiralled up in front of her face.

'You're smoking?' She just smiled. 'I've never seen you smoking.'

'You really don't know anything about me, Joe.' Her voice was slurred; she had probably had a few glasses of wine.

'Don't I?'

'No.'

'Maybe there aren't many people who really know about you. Maybe you prefer it like that?'

She laughed.

'Been here long?' I asked, standing close.

'I've been cutting down an old birch tree which was over-hanging the roof,' she replied, 'and I've cut up some wood. Then I heated a lamb casserole in the oven and opened a bottle of wine.' She looked at me with a flirtatious expression. 'You're so damned ugly,' she said. I felt a rising tingle of excitement. 'You were ugly even as a child,' she said, 'but

29

you're much worse now, more wrinkled. You look like a sick dog.'

I liked her smile and her hoarse voice. 'Were you expecting me?'

She shook her head, and her dark hair fluttered round her face. She threw the cigarette away into the grass. I sat down beside her on the step. I wanted to kiss her and feel her exploring tongue glide into my mouth. I wanted to feel her hands against my body.

'I was hoping you would be here,' I said.

'Why was that?'

'I haven't seen you for weeks. I like to look at you. I like to talk with you.'

She wriggled her bare toes on the step. 'I'm so tired,' she said.

'Why?'

She looked away.

'I met Vebjorn,' I said, 'in the supermarket.'

'So what did he say?'

'Not very much.' I put my hand on her shoulder and felt her warm skin against my palm. She smelled of smoke and liquorice.

'I haven't got round to reading your book yet.'

'That's alright.'

'It's inside there, on the bedside table. I'd thought of starting it this evening.' She blinked, and for a moment I thought she was going to start crying.

'Do you often think about me, Joe? When you shut your eyes, do you see my face?'

I felt myself shiver. 'Why are you asking that?'

'I want to leave him. I think so. I can't take it any more.'

'Has something happened?'

She shook her head. 'No, but he knows there's something wrong. He's dragging a great load of anger. He's like a wounded beast every time he comes home.'

'What does he say?'

'Not a word. That's the worst of it. I'm getting scared. He just sits there brooding. Won't talk, won't say anything. It's like when he went so bloody paranoid, right at the end of his time in Telemark.'

Katinka and I started seeing each other while Vebjorn was inside. He got out early in February and immediately moved into the terraced house in Frysja with her. But something had happened to him in prison. He had become a remote, angry man, she said. When he went in, he was just a novice who grew pot and thought he was king of the castle.

'I can't stop thinking about you,' I whispered, kissing her neck. 'I try, but I just can't. I keep coming back. I meant to run on past the hut this evening, but it didn't work out like that.'

She leaned her head back. Her neck was long and strong. 'I don't like that damned full moon.'

I turned. I hadn't seen the moon. While I was running on the hillside, the spruce trees had closed me in.

'It's as if there's someone staring at me.'

I looked at the gap between her front teeth, unable to hold my gaze away from her lips and mouth. Didn't just want to kiss her. Wanted to pull her right into me and feel her sharp nipples against my chest and the moisture between her thighs. I wanted to go right into her and through her.

She put her hand to her mouth. 'What are you staring at?'

I shrugged my shoulders.

'It's chilly,' she continued. 'Shall we go in?'

I followed her into the hut and as soon as I closed the door behind us, she grabbed hold of me and dragged me with her. She shoved me down onto the bed and threw her clothes onto the floor.

Her body was wildly beautiful.

She pulled off my tracksuit bottoms and took hold of my prick, slowly wanked me as she looked in my eyes and

31

tenderly called me *scarecrow, scarecrow*. I gasped for breath. She bent down over me and gently bit me up the length of my shaft and called me *scarecrow* and I glimpsed her white teeth against the head, and then she sunk her mouth down over the head and I shut my eyes and felt my prick sliding further and further into her mouth, and I think I heard her voice whispering *scarecrow, scarecrow*, and the tears welled up in my eyes and then everything went black and I felt as if I was going to faint.

When I got back to the station, the lights at the station house were on and the car was bathed in yellow light. The wind was rustling the bushes, and the branches were scraping against the side of the old party bus which had been abandoned there. Through the glass door I could see dark seats, plastic bags, soft drink cans and old chocolate papers on the floor.

In the car I thought about Katinka's mouth and the smell of her cigarette smoke. My fingers were trembling as I found the car keys, dropped them on the floor and had to bend down to scrabble for them in the dark.

I opened the window and drew in the cool air from the woods. Drove away from Sandermosen Station, back towards Frysja.

Through the side window I peeped into cul-de-sacs and gardens and garage doors. We had bathed in the river and played croquet on these lawns, played cowboys and Indians and put up our tent in Iver's big garden. I had been at a class party at Elin's and watched her undressing in a broom cupboard. I remembered her white thighs and the little cleft between them.

In the dark of winter I stood on the bridge and threw lumps of ice into the darkness, watched them disappear and waited for the sound of them hitting the hard-packed ice, unseen.

Dusk came down over the shadowy hedges, like gaps between the lawns, tiny little chasms with dark edges. The

32

pegs of a tent had come loose from a lawn, and the fabric of the tent was fluttering in the wind.

I drove on past the gardens, the paved terraces and the double garages. Frysja had changed. All the old craftsmen and manual workers had gone, their houses taken over by businessmen and doctors and brokers with *nouveau riche* tastes and fickle smiles. I didn't feel I belonged any more.

Our sense of innocence is cynical. We know the world is rotten, but we pretend that nothing has changed. We bathe in the river. We put up a tent in the garden for our children. Jog on the trails under swaying tree tops.

The sound of a train came closer; a whistle echoed through the landscape. I drove up in front of the crooked old house that my father had once been so proud of and sat for a few seconds. Thinking of his occasional slanting smile, I remembered something else and saw it clearly.

I was standing in my room, looking out over the road. Dad's car drove up in front of the fence and the engine stopped, but he didn't come out. Instead, he sat with his hands on the wheel, staring ahead. It was as if he was readying himself for a really difficult task. I held my breath as I watched him, and felt that I was looking into something I was not supposed to see.

Why was he sitting motionless?

What was he getting ready for?

Why was he so quiet?

Was it because he was tired of all the coffins and dead bodies? Whenever I went to see him at the office, I wondered what it would be like to take over his job, as he had from grandfather. What would *I* be like if I worked with coffins and dead bodies every single day? Would I be as quiet?

My mobile phone on the passenger seat gave a buzzing sound. A new message. Unknown number. I pressed the message key. A picture came up, taken with a telephoto lens; the faces were close together, Katinka's mouth half open,

33

mid through a sentence. My hands were twisting through her hair.

I yelled at the windscreen, and the sound reverberated like a landslide through the car.

Sooner or later I'm going to fall. I know that, and I dread it. Yet I still go right to the edge of the pit, even though I know that I'm going to be dizzy and sick and feel an urge to jump. I still go right to the edge, shut my eyes and lean over before turning and walking away, already dreading coming back and knowing that it will not be long before I have again found the path through the woods and walked for hours without stopping to get to the very place where I hate and love to be.

All was quiet in the house, just as it should be at ten past eleven. Agnes was asleep.

I showered, lathered my hair, thought of Katinka, thought I could still smell the smoky aroma from her mouth. Then I sat in the dark in the living room with my mobile in my hands, staring at the picture of the two people sitting on the step in front of the hut.

Rain ran down the windows, and I imagined it oozing in through the cracks in the house walls and streaming over the floor. I deleted the message, but sat for a while with the mobile in my hand before switching off.

Up on Grefsen Hill, a light was moving slowly over the tree tops.

Who the hell had followed me to Sandermosen? A private investigator, I reckoned, some bloody private investigator hired by Agnes. I went into the bedroom. The contour of her face was silhouetted against the black pillow.

How long had she known about my relationship with Katinka? How long had she had suspicions? I stood at the side of the bed and looked down. What sort of private investigator would she hire? What had she been thinking when she called him?

Quick, angry fingers key the number. It begins to ring. A voice answers.

'Hello, this is Morten, private investigator.'

'Have you found him?' *she asks.* 'Was he with the whore?'

No, it couldn't be like that.

Vebjorn, I thought, and immediately got this feeling that somebody was watching me, that there was someone in the garden peeping in. I went over to the bedroom window and looked out. Something moved in the bushes, someone trying to creep backwards out of the garden without being seen. I ran through the living room and out through the terrace door, ran through the wet grass to the dark bushes and drew the branches aside.

'Vebjorn?'

I stared in through the tangle of branches: nothing there. Raindrops fell on my neck. I looked up at the bedroom window, where I had been a moment before.

I had blundered. I should never have contacted her, taken coffee with her in the café in Grefsen Street. I should have known that it would not work out well.

As I entered the living room again, I heard the faint buzz from the extra mobile phone which I had hidden in an inner pocket. I dug it out and answered her, but couldn't hear anything at the other end. I tried to call back; no contact: *The subscriber has switched off the phone or is in a zone with no signal.*

Putting the phone back in my inner pocket I wondered whether I should go running again tomorrow.

5

I do love Agnes, I said to myself. I had never thought of myself as an unfaithful husband, but that's what I was; a cowardly liar who sneaked through the woods late in the evening to visit his whorish lover. I had always thought of myself as loyal and honourable, but when I kissed Katinka and immediately felt the urge to lay her, I was struck by how naturally the act of betrayal followed. It seemed to be an aptitude I had always possessed, further developed in secret, but never made use of. I knew how to betray, tell lies and cover my tracks. It wasn't something I had to learn by experience. It came easily.

The concealment programme, the extra telephone, the lie and the smile which covered up the kissing and the fucking and the unfaithfulness were like a game remembered from childhood which I had remastered after just a few minutes. It was frightening to see how easily an apparently well balanced and amiable man changed into a treacherous, egotistic monster.

A single meeting in a coffee bar was all it took to split us from the harmony which had characterised our life together. Sure, we had argued and there had been times when our relationship didn't work well, but these disagreements were relatively minor. A few months after I started my affair with Katinka, I realised that life with Agnes had become a double game. Of course, she noticed that I was in a low patch, that I was distant and behaving oddly, but she couldn't have recognised my intense feeling of self-contempt.

A suicide bomber motivated by love, I had tied the explosives round my waist and marched right into our house where I sat in the living room with Emma and Agnes, watching TV and waiting for the explosion which would tear us all to shreds. I'm exaggerating, but I *felt* like a terrorist bent on destruction.

'What are you thinking about?' Agnes asked over breakfast on Thursday morning.

'Nothing, love.' I shook my head absent-mindedly. 'Can you pass me the orange juice?' I filled the glass to the brim, raised it to my lips and drank. Too acid, I thought, as if past its date. Was I just imagining that rotten taste in my mouth? I swallowed, and felt the juice run down to my stomach.

'What'll we do today, Daddy?' Emma squeezed some fish paste out of the tube onto a half slice of bread. 'It's raining,' she said, looking forlornly out of the window.

'We can go to the cinema,' I said, putting my glass down again.

'What film will we see, Mummy?'

Agnes hadn't taken her eyes off me. 'I think I'll stay at home.'

'Why?' Emma asked.

'I've got a headache.'

'It doesn't matter,' I said to Emma with a smile. 'You and I can go to the cinema.'

'Can we?'

'Sure we can.' I looked at Agnes. Was it my imagination, or had something hard and distant appeared in her face? Lies are strange things, I thought. They develop unseen and lead to complications even if they are never discovered.

Agnes went back to the bedroom and drew the curtains.

Emma and I said nothing for a few minutes as we drove into town. Eventually I broke the silence: 'What sort of film would you like to see?'

'A film about vampires.'

'That's not for children.'

'Vera Linn says it's fun.'

Vera Linn was her best friend from nursery school. I tried unsuccessfully to remember what she looked like. Was her hair light or dark? Vera Linn. The name reminded me of somebody. Wasn't there a British singer called Vera Linn? The one who sang the old hit 'We'll meet again'. I tried to envisage the little girl's face. Emma and Vera Linn. Emma was fair. Vera Linn was dark. She had short, clipped hair and sly eyes. The pair of them were standing in the square in front of the nursery school in knee-length frocks, hand in hand and silent, in front of the swing which was swaying back and forward. There was a little boy lying face down in the sand.

We found a film eventually. Emma liked it, she told me afterwards, but I don't remember much about it. I was too busy wondering what Katinka had wanted to tell me when we were cut off. Not really with it, I felt that my thoughts were detached and hovering around her hut while my body sat restlessly in the cinema beside Emma. I couldn't relax properly until I knew why she had tried to call.

In the car on the way home I considered the various options of lie, and which would be most credible. My cousin Jenny had recently moved into a flat in Nydalen. I could say that I had to take something to her. But that was too risky, Agnes and Jenny spoke to each other on the phone now and again. If anything happened while I was away, Agnes might think of phoning Jenny and it would seem strange that Jenny hadn't had the delivery. Oh, my God, Jenny was a detective, naturally suspicious. What on Earth was I thinking?

I didn't find the perfect lie, but I did feel more relaxed. Thinking about it had helped me regain control. Perhaps, I thought in a microsecond of calm, this is the beginning of the end. Perhaps she will tell me that we can't go on; that she is frightened Vebjorn will find us out and that I can't come to her hut any more.

On Thursday evening I felt relaxed. I made dinner for the girls and was in a better mood than I had been for a long time. When I poured wine into Agnes's glass, I caught an amazed expression on her face. It was a long time since she had seen me so cheerful.

6

'Daddy, you sleepyhead!'

I blinked, and saw Emma looking down at me from the side of the bed, her long, fair hair like a curtain over her face. The space beside me was empty. It was Sunday morning: more than twenty four hours since the message on my phone and my run around the garden looking for someone who wasn't there.

'Where's Mummy?' She didn't reply. 'Emma?'

'She went out for a little morning walk.'

I looked at the clock on the bedside table. It was after 9.00 am. I didn't usually sleep so late.

'She's waiting for you.'

I wiped the sleep out of my eyes. 'Who?'

'Didn't you hear it?'

'What?'

'The door-bell, *ding-dong*.' She was wearing her *Hello Kitty* pyjamas and I thought there was something malevolent and insincere about the cat's eyes. 'The police lady. She wants to talk to you.'

I sat up. My neck felt stiff; I had been lying in an awkward position. Where on earth was Agnes, I wondered. 'A police lady?'

A little smile glimmered in her mouth. Was this some game she had invented? I held her and drew her towards me. 'You're not making up stories, are you? You remember what happened to the boy who cried "wolf."' She nodded. 'He got eaten up.'

'Daddy, she's out there waiting for you.'

'Really?'

'Yes, really!'

I pulled on my old dressing gown. The rain had been drumming on the window for hours, intruding into my dreams. Now it was quiet. Emma had left the front door open. Standing on the step was a sinewy, slender woman in a leather jacket.

'Hi, Joe.' It was Thea Dalen, Jenny's assistant.

'I've just got up,' I said, glancing down at the dressing gown's loose threads dangling in front of my knobbly knees.

'Jenny's waiting for you in the car.' Thea nodded towards the yard and an unmarked police car parked there. I recognised Jenny's head behind the misted windscreen.

'What's going on? Why didn't she call me herself?'

Thea looked me up and down as if she was assessing the trustworthiness of some very persistent complainant. 'She had to take a phone call.'

What the hell was going on? Jenny was bending over the steering wheel, listening intently to her mobile. Under her black forelock, her eyes were closed.

Jenny and I had lived just a stone's throw from each other all the time we were growing up, she in Radioveien when I was in Frysjaveien. Our fathers ran the funeral business together, having taken the business over from their father, Knut Uddermann, who had been an active and efficient undertaker since 1933. The old man died at only sixty four, soon after the sons took over. I once heard my Dad say: *He coffined himself.* Dad was a calm, courteous, quiet and introspective man except when he drank whisky. It was as if another being lived inside him. Then he used a voice which frightened me out of my wits, a varying dark and light, cursing, pleading and pathetic voice. I often ran barefoot in the night to Jenny's house when he was holding forth and I couldn't sleep.

Aunt Vera used to let me in without saying a word, and I would scurry along the passage to Jenny's room and into her warm bed. She would pull me in, without asking what had happened, and I would lay my face against her big, warm shoulder and fall asleep.

'I'll put on my trousers,' I told Thea, and went back to the bedroom to find some clothes.

'Two minutes!' she called, in an irritating, nasal tone.

As soon as I sat in the car, I knew something was seriously wrong. Jenny hugged me as usual and kissed my cheek, as she had done since I was a child, but her smile had a gloomy look. Four years older than me, she said I was her substitute little brother and, when she kissed me, I felt that the world could hold together despite everything.

'Do you realise what time it is?' I asked.

She glanced down at the mobile in her hand. One message, several question marks.

'What's going on?

'Glad to see you, cousin,' she said.

Behind her fixed expression I could still see the girl who comfort ate and did weight training to develop herself. Already big as a teenager, she had grown in height and breadth, had muscles like a man and trained for kickboxing and karate. When I was a skinny, fearful little chap with glasses I thought she was huge, and it seemed quite natural when she joined the police, even though she came from a family of undertakers. Nobody messed with Jenny!

Some look after the living, others look after the dead.

'It's early Sunday morning, Jenny. What's up?'

She stared at the road. The morning mist had come in again. Thea was standing under the lilac bush talking into her mobile phone.

My imagination glimpsed the text message again, with the picture of two people on the step in front of the timber hut. 'I

42

was sleeping so soundly,' I said. 'For the first time in weeks I was sleeping like a babe. Then Emma came to waken me and said there was a police lady at the door.'

She smiled, but with difficulty, and shook her head. 'It's an ugly business.' She stroked a dark lock of hair from her forehead.

'What on earth are you talking about?'

She pursed her lips as she usually did when she didn't like something, then told me about a wooden chest found in the woods on the morning of the previous day, Saturday.

'Someone out walking found it, right in the middle of the woods. A typical old rose-painted chest like many in Norwegian huts, but this one was in the middle of a bog. It was a man in his fifties, a Norwegian teacher at Engebraten School, whose dog discovered the chest. Barked like mad. He opened it and phoned us right away. It was the worst thing he had ever seen, he said. She was completely naked.'

'Why are you telling me this, Jenny?' She didn't answer. 'Why are you here?'

'Katinka Moen.'

It was like a heavy punch in the stomach. 'What's up with her?'

She looked me in the face and said quietly, 'She's been murdered.'

I shook my head.

'That's who was in the chest. She was found right beside her family's old hut.'

The asphalt was wet with rain. 'Are you sure it's Katinka?'

She nodded.

'I feel sick,' I said, frightened that I might throw up. 'When did it happen?'

'Probably Friday night, possibly early Saturday morning.'

I shut my eyes and visualised Katinka's naked body curled up in a chest. Out on the road, Thea turned towards the car.

'We found something else in the chest,' Jenny said. She

opened a file and handed me a torn off page of a book, inside a plastic folder. The sheet had obviously been rolled up and opened out again. At the foot of the page was the number 29. At the top was the title of the book: *The Chalk*. The rest of the page was covered with dense prose, typeset in New Baskerville and printed on 90 gram Munken Print Cream. I didn't need to read it. It was from Chapter Three.

I returned the plastic folder, feeling as if a sharp object was being dragged out of my guts. 'What does it mean? Where did you find it?'

'Inside her mouth.'

'In her mouth?'

She looked at me carefully. 'Are you OK?'

I tried to nod.

'Did you give her that book?'

'Yes. She was helping me with the research.'

'And?'

'And so I gave her a copy of the book.'

Jenny's mobile phone began to squeal. She looked at the screen.

'I need to go. Can you come to the police station and give us a statement?'

'When?'

'I'll send you an appointment, OK?'

I mumbled 'Yes' and imagined Katinka's face, with the little gap between her teeth. Overcome by a wave of nausea, I threw the car door open and spewed over the asphalt. 'Excuse me,' I mumbled as I scrambled out.

Agnes came walking down the road, wearing a raincoat and big waterproof boots. She stopped, and I looked across at her. The Volvo drove past.

'What's going on?' she asked. I looked down at her boots. 'What's up?'

I took a deep breath and told her what Jenny had said, but

she didn't meet my look. It was as if she wasn't listening.

'Are you listening?'

'What?' Her eyes were as grey as the surrounding mist.

'Katinka is dead …' My voice broke.

'Dead?'

Her gaze fixed on the flakes of mist and didn't come back.

I put my arms around her, but she had gone stiff. 'It's dreadful,' I whispered.

I felt the touch of her lips against my ear. 'Was she murdered?'

I nodded.

Agnes wriggled out of my arms to run into the house and I sat down on the driveway, without the strength to get up. I lay right back on the ground, put my head back, banged it on a small stone and thought of Katinka's smile.

It's as if there's someone staring at me.

Agnes's boots lay on the floor in the hallway where Emma stood waiting. 'What's up with Mummy?' Her arms were folded tightly across her chest.

'Everything's out of step,' I mumbled.

'What?'

I patted her head.

'Daddy, say what it is.'

'Somebody's dead,' I said. She asked who it was and I said that it was someone that Mummy and I knew.

'But who?'

'Somebody we went to school with.'

'In the olden days?'

'Yes.'

'But who?'

'A lady called Katinka, a friend of Mummy's.'

'Katinka?' I nodded. 'Have I met her?'

I kneeled down. Little white dots flickered on the tiles. I couldn't remember whether Emma had met Katinka. She

45

must have done, one time or another. Soon after Emma was born? An old memory rose from deep in my consciousness, a conversation, something Agnes said about Katinka the first time she saw Emma. Hadn't Agnes said something like: *She doesn't like children.*

'Has she been killed?' Emma stroked my cheek.

I looked at her pale face and said that I didn't know, but I thought so. We went through to the living room where Agnes was sitting on the sofa, staring straight ahead like a doll.

'Katinka is dead,' Emma said with a sad face.

Agnes nodded. 'I just want to sit peacefully for a while.'

I poured some cornflakes for Emma and turned the radio on. Lana del Rey was singing *Video Games.* I smiled, and realised I was crying. I rinsed my face in warm water. 'I feel so cold.'

Emma gave me a strange look. 'It's not cold here, Daddy.'

'Isn't it?'

She shook her head and ate the rest of the cornflakes. 'Can I watch a film? Because it's Sunday?'

I lay on the bed with my eyes closed. The room temperature seemed to drop, as if I was lying at the bottom of a freezer. Agnes was still in the living room. Why wouldn't she speak? Why just sit there thinking? Emma was in the downstairs room. I could hear the film music, a high-pitched, out of tune Tyrolean music.

I couldn't manage to get up from the bed.

The music stopped.

My fingers so cold they were painful.

Katinka said she was tired. She was going to get a divorce, she said. Did she really mean that? I remembered the smoke blowing from her lips. He's killing me, she said. The air felt cold and I thought that I was being enclosed in a little, cold space. I sat up and rocked back and forwards.

Edgar Allan Poe wrote about the demons in whose

46

company Afrasiab made his voyage down the Oxus: *they must sleep, or they will devour us -- they must be suffered to slumber, or we perish.*

My thoughts were whirling demons.I closed my eyes, and saw her roguish smile.

'Do you often think about me, Joe? When you shut your eyes, do you see my face then?'

I looked up. Agnes was standing at the foot of the bed.

'What's wrong with you?' She bent down towards me. 'Are you crying?'

I sat up, dizzy. 'What?'

She walked round the end of the bed and sat on the edge, laid her fingertips on my face. 'Are you crying?'

I laid her hands against my cheeks. 'I was sleeping … and …'

Her fingertips were wet.

'You were lying there weeping.' I couldn't speak. 'Have you been with Katinka?'

I stared at a little mark on the skin between her eyes. 'What?'

'Just answer me, Joe,' she whispered.

'Where did you get that ridiculous idea from?'

She bit her lower lip, and the skin around her mouth turned a flaming violet colour.

'You lie here weeping and you've been behaving so damned oddly, and every time I say her name your face turns chalk white. Joe, I know there's something wrong, do you think I don't know there's somebody else? Do you think I haven't noticed?'

Wild guesswork, I thought. No evidence. 'What are you talking about, Agnes?'

'Stop!'

'What? I don't know what you're talking about. You come rushing into the room and fling a heap of accusations at me. *Dear God!* She's been murdered. What in hell's name has put such thoughts into your head?'

She rose from the bed and stood motionless, and for a moment I thought she had given up, that nothing more would come of it and that the wave of suspicion would recede.

'Do you really think,' she said in a worryingly restrained tone, 'that I haven't seen through you?'

I opened my mouth to speak but she held up a warning hand.

'Please, Joe, don't say any more. You just seem so pathetic. I know you're lying. Every word you say is false. Do you really believe I don't see it in your face too? What do you think of me? Do you think I don't care?'

I couldn't look at her. If I said something wrong there would be no way back. Take a deep breath. Think. Don't look at her. Wait.

'I've known for a long time that there was something going on.' I nodded. 'But I didn't realise ...' Her hair fell over her eyes. 'God! I'll have to sit down.'

She sat again on the bed. One arm fell between us and hung limp over the edge. It was as if she was worn out and had nothing more to give.

I looked at her naked knees. 'You,' I said.

'What?'

'You're right.'

She looked at me, her eyes moist.

I wiped my forehead. 'You know that time I met her – to ask her about a chapter in my book?' She nodded. 'Something happened. Not then, but soon after. Quite by accident. Up in her hut.'

'At the hut?'

'I go running up there.'

'Past her hut?'

'Yes. And one evening she was standing outside, and we started talking and ... yes, one thing led to another.'

48

'I don't want to hear any more.'

'It was just that one time, Agnes.'

She jumped up again from the bed. 'Just once?'

'I love you,' I said, and stood up. We stood facing each other and I looked directly at her face. 'I disgraced myself. I didn't know how to tell you what had happened. It was just a mistake, you understand? Nothing serious.'

'Just once?'

I nodded.

'Just the one time.'

I didn't see the blow coming which hit me right on the ear and knocked me backwards against the wall. The heat and the pain spread over my ear. I saw her face above me, yelling something that I couldn't make out.

Then the bedroom door slammed again, and nothing could be put right.

She slept on the living room sofa that night, and I lay in the bedroom listening to her whimpering and mumbling. In the middle of the night I awakened and heard her shuffling backwards and forwards. By the next morning she had packed two big suitcases.

'We're moving to my Dad's house,' she said, dragging the cases towards the door. Agnes's father lived at Solemskogen, not far away.

'Shall I drive you there?'

'Keep away from me,' she whispered with a hatred in her voice which was as foreign to her as it was overwhelming. 'I've got my own car.'

When I bent down to help her lift the biggest of the suitcases, she spat in my face. I stumbled and fell over the gumboots and landed with a raincoat on top of me.

Emma was still asleep, and so Agnes had to waken her.

'Where are we going, Mummy?'

'To Granddad's house.'

'Why?'

She looked at me over Agnes's shoulder as Agnes carried her out to the car. I raised my hand and waved. 'Emma... I ...'

The car door shut and the engine started and I descended to the cellar to sit on a chair and yell at the brick wall until my voice failed.

7

My parents died on a holiday trip to Tanzania in 2006 and the house in Frysjaveien stood empty for over a year.

Bothered by the thought of what they would have said about selling, at the same time I hesitated to move back in. Creeping back into too restricted an environment I might get stuck and never get out again. Maybe most people don't like to admit that we are very like our parents, not just in how we make choices but also in how we think and subconsciously make decisions we ought not to have made.

Agnes was quite sure that it would be good to take over the house. 'Don't be scared,' she said with an inscrutably optimistic smile. 'It'll be fine.'

The suggestion that I was scared bothered me, and led me to think everything afresh. In the end Agnes's powers of persuasion won me over and I came to believe that I would find peace of mind.

At that time we lived in a small flat in Torshov. Agnes had finished her legal studies and begun to look for a job. I had written my first novel and was well into the second. Agnes is right, I thought. We needed more space, and would have to find a new house sooner or later. I decided to trust her optimism and we moved to Frysja, to the 'safe place' where I had grown up but that I had decided, many years before, never to move back to.

Emma was a year and a half when we moved in. She had begun to sleep at night and we had passed the most stressful

51

phase of being parents. Life as house owners was a new experience for us though, and we didn't know how to deal with the leak which, drop by drop, was turning the basement into a clammy grotto. We pitched in to what had to be done, and cleared away all the old things left from my mother and father's day. New possibilities opened up as we threw furniture into the skip.

Deciding to renovate, I wanted to make a thorough job of it. As I had sold our share of the funeral business to Uncle Sven, I had money to spend. We laid new floors in the living room and kitchen, got rid of the old kitchen cupboards and installed a new bathroom. We replaced all the old furniture, and I began to believe that I would adjust to life in a villa.

Jenny said, 'You wouldn't recognise this house', but it was only internally that everything was different. Externally it looked exactly the same and I felt as if I had put on my father's old suit and couldn't take it off again. I had become a house and garden owner. I had never imagined that I would end up as a garden owner. There was something frightening about the idea.

Agnes had a good laugh when I told her. 'Are you scared of the garden?'

I was standing in the hallway with my hands covered in soil. We had been planting Emma's plum tree. 'Terrified.' I had always been frightened of a garden troll, ever since as a young boy I lay in bed with the window open and thought I heard somebody sneaking around among the apple trees, a huge man with his fists full of soil.

She laughed and kissed me.

For the whole of the first year Agnes was irrepressibly positive and energetic. She glowed, and I felt lucky. We went for long walks along the river with Emma. Those were our best times.

Agnes and I had now been living together in Frysjaveien for five years. We had made the house our own, an author and

52

a lawyer and a little fair-haired girl with a quaint, crooked smile. When did it start to go wrong? Was it my phone call to Katinka, or was it the day I met her in the café?

Or was it on a warm September evening, two weeks later? Agnes and I were sitting in the garden enjoying a bottle of wine. It was a Saturday, one of those September days which in Norway make you feel that you are especially lucky because summer has been extended, autumn is delayed and winter is still a long way ahead. The temperature had been 25°. We had covered ourselves with sun cream and were lounging in the garden. I had fixed up a hammock between the branches of the old apple trees, and Emma had lain in it playing with her Barbie dolls and telling them stories in a sun-drowsed voice. Now she was asleep in our bedroom and we had opened a second bottle of red wine. Agnes's voice took on a stinging tone. She could say horrible things when she had been drinking.

She reached for the lighter and lit another cigarette without shifting her destructive look from me. She had a 'strange feeling,' she said, when she had gone back into our house earlier that day. Smoke seeped out between her lips.

'What was that?'

'That you had been with someone else.'

'That I had been with someone? What do you mean?'

'That you – just then – while I was walking towards the house, were lying there fucking somebody in our bed.

'I didn't know that you were so pathologically jealous.'

'I'm not jealous. It was just an idea I had.' It seemed as if she wanted me to say something.

'It sounds as if you were hoping to catch me out.'

'Does it?' She smiled, bitterly, her front teeth darkened by the wine. 'I even stopped in front of the door, walked back into the garden and looked in through our bedroom window. It was dark in there, but just as I stretched up to look in I thought I saw something in the bed. Two bodies:

your body; and a dark body, an African lady you were busily fucking.'

'Stop it!' This wasn't funny.

'But it was nothing.'

'No.' I put down my wineglass. *Busily fucking*. I felt sick. 'Why do you say such things?'

'Because that's what it's like,' she replied.

'What is like that?'

'Looking through our bedroom window.'

'Did you really think that I was in bed with someone else?' She scrutinised me seriously. 'I don't trust you.'

'Why do you say that?'

She stubbed out her cigarette. 'There's another side to you.'

'Another side?'

There were tears in her eyes. 'Do you really think I haven't seen through you?' I know that you're going with someone else.'

'Who?'

'I don't know.'

What had started as a game suddenly became serious. I didn't know what to say and just blurted something incoherent, but the strange thing was that her guess was correct. I hadn't been unfaithful. Not then, not yet, but I had fantasised about it.

Every time I ran past Katinka's hut I imagined myself lying with her in one of the narrow bunk beds, both of us naked. I was licking her nipples, her belly, her navel. As I ran through the woods, the picture was like a memory, as if I had actually been in the bunk bed a few days before but didn't want to admit it.

8

It was getting dark when I came up from the basement. For a few minutes I watched the light fade over Grefsen Hill and the rooftops of the houses on the hillside. My hand tightened so hard round the car keys that it was painful. I drove along the gravel road towards Sandermosen Station, trying not to think about Agnes and the reasons we were no longer together.

The spruce woods on either side of the road were dense, with branches and stems and moss and spiders' webs intertwined into an impenetrable, dark mass. The woods opened out at last onto a river bed, and between the trees I caught sight of the yellow painted station building. I drove over the railway track and thought I heard the whistle of a train further up the valley. The old party bus was still there at the edge of the wood, decaying and rusty. The barrier was open, and I drove a few hundred metres up the forest track before parking in a little clearing which couldn't be seen from the road. Three police vehicles were parked with their lights on about a hundred metres ahead.

It was raining hard, and I pulled the hood of my waterproof jacket well down over my face.

A tortuous path wound through the woods towards the Moen family's hut. I followed it through the dark, treading carefully on the stones, to the old birch tree where I could peer in.

*

A dog returns to its vomit. A human picks at a wound before it is healed, knocks the scab off and explores it with persistent, childish curiosity.

The police had sealed off the area. In the darkness, I could see Thea Dalen standing at the building and talking to two forensic technicians. The beam of a powerful torch swept over the building and the police officers and settled on the entrance door. A figure clad in waterproofs crossed the space, a torch in hand, and now I could see Jenny's face from the side. She walked over to Thea and the technicians. The light from her torch reflected off the assistant's face like light from the face of the moon. I heard their voices faintly.

'*What have you found?*'

'*A book. On her bedside table.*'

'*A book?*'

'*Joe Uddermann.*'

I caught sight of a transparent plastic bag between their arms, and I could see immediately what was in it: the novel which I had given to Katinka. The cover was torn to pieces, as if it had been trampled on. I remembered that I had written in it a dedication to her. 'THANK YOU.' Just the two words, together with my initials.

'*OK. Anything else?*'

'*A few stains.*'

'*On the book?*'

'*Yes. We can easily check them against both her husband and the author.*'

I drew back behind the birch tree. It was too late to go forward now. I had thought of talking to Jenny to tell her that I had been in the hut and that Katinka and I had had a relationship, but it was too late now.

Thea's quiet voice came across the clearing.

I imagined Katinka's face. She was smiling. I wanted to kiss her so that I could once again feel her smooth, pointed, penetrating tongue. I turned back carefully in the dark and after thirty metres started running towards the road.

I was soaking wet when I got home. I changed my clothes, made a cup of tea and sat on the living room sofa with only the reading lamp on. I looked through an old photo album. The picture I was looking for, of Agnes and me, had come loose from the page and been shoved into the back of the album. It was from a trip we made to the hills after we finished senior high school. Sitting against the wall of a hut we were trying not to laugh.

I had studied that picture many, many times, always trying to remember what we had been laughing at. I couldn't take my eyes off our youthful faces. Why were we so happy? I lifted the picture up to the light, shut my eyes and tried to think.

Easter. Sunshine in our faces.

What were we laughing at?

Was it because the delay timer on our camera repeatedly took the picture too soon, so that I didn't reach the hut wall in time to take up a convincingly natural position? No. It wasn't the camera we were laughing at, though it did play some part in our hilarity.

It wasn't 'the-secret-of-what-we-were-laughing-at' which made me bring out the photo again and again. It was the innocence in our faces, the lively and spontaneous smiles.

'What are we laughing at?' I had asked Agnes several times.

She just shrugged her shoulders. 'You've asked about that before.'

'Have I?'

'Yes. Several times.'

'Don't you remember?' I held the picture up to her.

'No.'

'Take a good look then."

She took the picture from my hand, held it to the light and studied it for a moment.

'Only silly old fogeys sit scrutinising photos of their bygone youth, Joe.'

I pretended I hadn't heard. 'Don't you remember?'

'No,' she said, handing the picture back with an air of indifference. 'I try to live in the present, Joe.'

Peering down at the picture, I suddenly recognised the similarity between them, Agnes and Katinka. They were really rather alike. Both had slightly slanting eyes. Straight noses. The eyebrows. Had the resemblance between them made Katinka even more attractive to me?

When I blinked, our faces melted into each other. Agnes, Katinka and my own face blended into a chaotic apparition.

'You're tired,' I mumbled to myself and put the photo album down.

Agnes was right. Leafing through old albums can put the healthiest brain off balance. I switched off the reading lamp knowing I must try to think logically about what had happened.

Who could have followed me to Sandermosen on Friday evening?

Who had a motive to kill Katinka? Agnes? Vebjorn?

Why had she been stuffed into a chest?

I thought of what Katinka had said about needing to start reading my book. The following morning she had been found crumpled into a chest in the woods.

Lovely, perfidious Katinka.

Thea Dalen had said that Vebjorn knew that she was unfaithful. Did he know who she was with?

Katinka was flirtatious. A stab in my chest; had she been with others?

Was it another lover? Someone who had seen me in front of the hut that evening? Someone who had lain in wait, plotting revenge against her? Someone who had been betrayed once too often?

Everything was out of joint. I thought of Vebjorn and the look in his eyes as he knocked me down in the supermarket.

He surely knew that I was an OK chap at heart?

Or was it the other way round? Did I have an OK surface but a foul heart?

'Shut up!' I yelled from the sofa, looking round as if someone might be listening behind a door or a curtain. I tried to visualise Vebjorn's face but it was blurred, out of focus. The fact was that I no longer knew who he was, what he had become. He had seemed unstable, I thought.

How angry was he? Enough to kill her? I didn't know.

The murderer knew her. I was sure about that. *A cunt with teeth*. Where the hell had I got that from? Was it something Agnes had said when she was half drunk?

They had been best friends. In the school playground Agnes always stood right behind Katinka. Agnes was the sensible one Katinka sought comfort from when she had been too cheeky and wilful.

Opposites attract each other, I thought. Agnes: sensible, reliable, ambitious. Katinka: cheeky, impulsive, flirtatious.

It wasn't self-evident that they would become friends, but they had been friends from nursery. At school they had clung to each other like twins, and it was not until their mid teens that they drifted apart. Katinka began to party with undesirable friends and cross boundaries which we others didn't want to cross. The boys in that gang were a bad lot, we said. They drank homemade spirits and took dope. They lived by trickery, sold pot, dodgy business. Agnes on the other hand was clever at school and had already decided to study law and didn't want to 'throw her life away partying.' Katinka wasn't afraid of throwing away anything, and she had no plans to go to university.

I closed my eyes and saw Katinka's face and the little gap between her front teeth. That dark space between her teeth. Along with Vebjorn she became more and more unpredictable, but she was beautiful too, and vulnerable and sad. Many people liked her, but she had broken too many hearts and betrayed too many friends. Agnes drew back and found other friends.

Then Agnes and I found each other.

The chest in the woods must have been from inside the hut. I remembered how Katinka kneeled against it with its rose paintings and monograms, offering her backside to me. I stood for a few seconds enjoying the sight of her naked, deep pink cleft until my prick became restless, as if there was an electric current flowing up the shaft – and then I remember her turning, looking at me over her shoulder and whispering: 'Fuck me properly then, you beast.'

Foul language streamed out of her pretty mouth with an intensity which startled me.

She laid her head back and cried out a prolonged *aaahhh* towards the roof of the hut. I didn't know whether she was making a fool of me or whether the porno talk was something she did for fun, or to see how I would react, or whether the dirty words gave her a feeling of slipping free from something. I don't know. I wasn't thinking clearly, because I was as randy and obedient as a dog and did exactly what she asked of me. I shoved in through her back door and filled the stinking little hole to breaking point. It felt so insanely good, spots danced before my eyes and I couldn't hold myself back. I chiselled my prick right into her and filled her up with my colourless, slimy spunk.

'*Stop it!*'

I drew the blanket up over my head.

Whoever had killed her had been in the hut, just as I had been. He too had lain naked on the sheepskin rugs in front of the stove and heard her whispering: 'You're so damned ugly, don't you know?'

I saw her mouth again.

'You're the ugliest man I've been with.' Her eyes were shining. 'I like your bony body too,' she said, sliding her fingers down over my belly.

'You look like a little boy. Everything sticks out on you. Even your prick is crooked and odd.'

'You're so sweet,' I whispered.

'No,' she said as she began kissing me down over my belly. 'I'm a dirty whore.'

Stop!

I sat up on the sofa and threw the blanket to the floor.

Think sensibly, for hell's sake!

I got up from the sofa and shuffled into the bedroom, my neck aching and my head thumping, not knowing whether I was on the right track or going up a muddy blind alley. Everything had gone wrong, and it was too late to find a solution for anything.

I swallowed a sleeping pill, crept under the duvet and curled into the foetal position. My head trembled. Katinka was sitting on the chest in the hut. She was naked and her skin glowed in the light from the paraffin lamp. Her face was swollen and she was crying. She mumbled something in a language I didn't understand.

Then I fell asleep.

I dreamt that I was a boy aged ten or eleven. My fringe of blond hair kept falling down over my forehead so that I was constantly stroking it away from my eyes.

I was walking through a dense wood at early dawn, wearing Dad's gumboots, which were too big for me, and his rain jacket which was also too big. I was like a miniature copy of him. The branches were bent over the path, heavy with rain as I walked along with stiff, manly steps. The sound of twigs cracking under my boots was subdued and sinister. I didn't know what I was looking for.

One boot got stuck in the bog. When I wrenched it loose

a foul smell seeped up from the hole. Soon the path disappeared. There was a deer standing in the clearing, gnawing the bark of a tree with small, rapid movements. I walked on further. Faint screams from the clearing. There was a wooden chest in the moss, a rose painted chest with iron fittings. The screams were coming from inside and I knew at once that this was what I was looking for. Fear tightened round my chest and I pinched my eyes again.

A gust of wind blew across my face. Soon it would begin to rain. I heard a robin singing overhead, and knew that the screams had ceased. I gazed at the chest. *It's all too quiet*, I thought as I opened the lock.

9

Barefoot in the garden I gazed towards the river. The mist had broken up, allowing sunlight to fall on the riverbank and the dark water. The dream was still swirling in my head, a residual feeling of constriction and dread and nausea. I could still feel the weight of the oversize rain jacket on my shoulders and hear the sounds inside the old chest.

In the kitchen I made a strong espresso.

Back in the garden I shut my eyes and sipped the coffee. The silence was broken by the sound of Agnes's car, a Golf with a whine from the fan belt.

She picked her way carefully into the garden as if she was worried that her trainers would sink through the turf and into the ancient muck under the lawn.

'It's a swamp here,' she muttered.

In the sharp morning light she seemed thinner, paler, more flushed round the eyes. I could see that she knew something I didn't. There was something in the way she stood, stiff and erect like an animal caught in the headlights of a lorry. She was so sensible, good at putting her thoughts into words, expressing her doubts, but when she was angry or very unhappy she stiffened up and couldn't say a word.

Who had she been talking to? Vebjorn? Had the two victims of betrayal been talking to each other? I felt that Vebjorn had said something to her, something vicious about me. Had he persuaded her that I was Katinka's murderer? Had he insinuated it, or said it right out? Was he so devious? Did he realise that Agnes was off balance? A hint that I was a swine, a beast, would find resonance in her. She was capable of believing the worst, full of suspicion, and all he had to do was hint at connections. She no longer knew what to believe. Right now he could get her to believe that I was anybody at all, for she no longer knew who on earth I was. She had trusted me, and now she didn't trust me, but did she trust Vebjorn?

Then I wasn't sure. I didn't even know whether she had spoken with him. Was it just something I had dreamed up? Wasn't it more likely that she had spoken with Jenny? 'Oh my God,' I mumbled.

Her eyes were blank.

'I can't bring myself to grasp what has happened,' I said tentatively.

She shook her head slowly, and her lips appeared to move.

'What did you say?'

She shook her head again.

'Who have you been speaking to?'

She didn't answer. 'I don't want to talk about it,' she whispered.

'Are you OK?'

'No.' She raised her hands defensively in the air. 'Don't bother me, please.' She put Emma's little case down on the ground between us and said tight-lipped: 'She's in the car.'

'What?'

'She wanted to go swimming, and I can't cope with that. I've not slept, not since ... I've called in sick. I haven't the strength to go swimming.'

'Don't worry. I can take her.'

'OK.'

That was a good sign, wasn't it? I was to take Emma swimming. She wouldn't send Emma out swimming with me if she believed I had done what Vebjorn wanted her to believe that I had done. Or would she? Was she just doing this to check up on me?

Would she really do that?

'I wanted to check first, that you could take her. And that you ... '

'What?'

She scrutinised me through her fringe of blonde hair.

'That I was OK?'

'Perhaps.'

I was about to say: 'That I wasn't a murderer as he had claimed?' but I held back. Tears were streaming down her cheeks. 'I'm sorry,' I murmured. 'Just forget it.'

Agnes cleared her throat and glanced down at the little case.

'She insisted on wearing her *Hello Kitty* swimming costume.'

I thought about the nursery school that Katinka and Agnes had gone to, together, near Stilla. I remembered two little girls hiding in a box in front of the red house. I stood by the fence, staring at the box and wondering what the two little girls were up to in there. Maybe I was a little bit in love with them even then, though I was only five?

'Have you spoken to Jenny?'

'Jenny?'

'Yes Jenny.' I didn't take my eyes off her.

'Only on the phone.'

'On the phone?'

'Yesterday evening.'

'What did she say?'

She didn't answer. Her lips were sealed.

They peeked out of the box through a slit, two mischievous little faces, and called quietly: *Nobody can find us.*

'You were at nursery school with her,' I said. She looked at me, warning me to stop. 'What did Jenny say? Did she say anything about me?'

'It's none of your business.' She stared at the house, avoiding my look.

65

'I dreamt that we had found her out in the woods,' I said, as I tipped the espresso onto the grass.

'It's hideous, that swimming costume,' she said quickly.

I looked down at my bare feet. A long, sticky blade of grass had attached itself to the outer side of my left foot. 'It didn't mean anything.'

'What?'

'What we did, Katinka and I.'

She gave me a cutting look. 'She's dead, Joe.'

'Hell, it wasn't me who killed her.'

A shaft of sunlight picked out her face. She looked down at the little puddle of coffee. 'What a swine you are, Joe. I didn't realise you were so bloody false. Really. Damn! I'm wading through muck here.' She looked down at her trainers. 'Hellish, shitty muck!'

I laid a hand on her shoulder. 'Try to get a little sleep.'

'Take your hands off me,' she protested, but she didn't draw back.

I pulled her in towards me, and she leaned against my chest. 'God, it's horrible,' I whispered. It sounded forced and strange. 'Love you,' I mumbled, but that sounded even stranger.

For a moment, we stood clasped together. The warmth from her forehead made its way through my t-shirt and into my skin. I wanted to scream, because I knew that this wouldn't last for more than a second, that this moment would then be over and she would go.

She murmured something I couldn't make out and broke loose.

The lawn was scruffy, like a matted and uncombed scalp. Grey, caked mud between tufts of grass made it a hideous caricature of a lawn. We had never got it as it should be. There was something wrong with the soil. I should have dug it all up and taken the soil away, replaced it with good topsoil and sown a completely new lawn.

I picked up Emma's little case.

Agnes had already walked into the shadow under the apple trees.

I called after her. 'Have you spoken to Emma about it?'

'I've told her what has happened.' It sounded like a threat.

'What do you mean?' I asked.

'What should I say to her?'

I shrugged. 'That everything will work out fine?'

She backed out of the garden. 'Go to hell,' she hissed, beginning to run.

The garden gate opened with a squeak, and Emma came running in. She jumped up to me and I gave her a hug.

'Why are you here alone?' she whispered in my ear.

'I don't know, treasure,' I said, giving her a kiss.

I heard the sound of the car starting.

Emma held the little case with her swimming costume in one hand and trundled her doll's pram with the other. Nora and Cindy and Ursula were sitting in the pram. The blonde figures were more than thirty years old, and their faces had acquired a pale yellowish colour. They had once belonged to Agnes, but now they lived in Emma's room. The three veteran long-legged blonde beauties had their own bed and make-up table and a red sports car. Inscrutable, half-smiling, cool, they jolted along in the pram.

'Daddy?'

'Yes dear.'

'What happens to people when they die?'

'Surely you know? They're buried.'

'In the ground?'

'Some …'

Ursula had had a leg amputated, just above the knee, and Cindy had lost both arms in an unexplained accident, but that didn't matter. They were as blonde as in their heyday, but it wasn't so easy now to do their hair with brush and comb.

Emma had once tried to sort out Cindy's hairstyle with the iron, but the hair stuck to the iron and black smoke poured up from her head. Now Cindy's hair was coal black on one side, but this didn't bring her into disfavour with her owner. I thought that was a good quality in a Barbie doll owner. Nora with her head aslant had also remained in favour. In Emma's eyes, Cindy and Nora and Ursula would always be beauties, no matter how ancient and ravaged they became.

'Some what?'

'Some are buried in coffins, as you know, but nowadays most are cremated. Their ashes are put into little boxes. Or urns.'

'Cremated?'

'They are burnt, my love.'

'On a bonfire?'

'No, not like that. In ovens.'

'Like buns?'

'No. These are bigger ovens.'

'How big?'

'Big.'

'Like a house.'

'No, not as big as that.'

She nodded, apparently satisfied with the answers, and trundled on down towards the river. 'We'll soon be there, and you'll get your morning bath,' she said to the three prima donnas in the pram. We went over the bridge to the bathing place, sunlight shining on the dolls' faces, and I spread out towels on the grass bank. It was only just past nine o'clock, and nobody else had come to bathe yet. By the time I got myself properly seated Emma had already changed into her *Hello Kitty* bathing costume.

'Aren't you going to swim too?'

I looked up at the hazy disc of the sun. 'I'll wait a little, till it warms up.'

She looked at me doubtfully. 'You're not going to swim at all today. You're just going to lie there quietly.'

I lifted my finger in the air as if I was feeling the wind. 'No, no. I will swim in a little while.'

'I don't believe that at all.' She walked resolutely towards the river.

'Five minutes ...,' I called after her, feeling a pang of guilt.

She held her head high and didn't turn back, wading until the water was up to her mid thighs. She stretched both arms in front of her, bent her knees, pushed herself out into the water and swam a couple of strokes. Then she did a quick turn and swam back. She cried out, water in her eyes, and I sprang up with the towel. She ran up the bank, shivering.

'What are you smiling about, you silly Daddy?'

'I'm smiling at you. Come along, I'll dry you.'

Her delicate body trembled between my hands. 'Was it cold, then?' Her teeth chattered. 'When it's a little warmer, we can go swimming together.' I gave her a hug.

'Maybe. I don't know if I'll bother.' She sat on the towel and started playing with the dolls.

I lay back, shut my eyes and felt the warm light of the sun on my skin. 'The sun's here at last,' I murmured.

'What?'

'The sun.'

Emma didn't reply. She went on talking gently to her dolls, already well into a new game.

I thought about the forensic technician with his white gloves, holding a plastic bag containing my novel.

I saw the book lying on Katinka's bedside table.

I saw her reading it, letter by letter.

Which page had she come to when she was interrupted?

What was she thinking of as she read?

My eyelids grew heavier.

Emma's whispering grew quieter.

When I woke up, all I could hear was the sound of the river.

69

10

For a few seconds I lay listening to the water rippling against the stones. It was refreshing to lie with my eyes shut, relaxing and imagining I was asleep. Then a car horn sounded on the road and I sat up with a jerk. The sunlight blinded me, and I held a hand up to my eyes. Emma was gone. There was nobody at the bathing place. I got up, dizzy after my short slumber.

'Emma?' I went down among the birch trees by the river's edge. 'Emma?'

The tree roots looked like children's arms in the green water. I was about to call out again when I spotted the case. Emma's little case was floating in the deep pool, drifting away.

As the water reached my waist I slipped on a stone, but got hold of the case and threw it on the bank. Then I dived to search under the water, along the stones and rushes and the pale tree-roots. Half-buried in the clay of the river bed was a stone the size of a head. I dived down, worked it loose from the clay, stood up with it in my hands and yelled her name again: 'Emma!'

I waded breathlessly back to the bank, sunshine stinging my eyes.

Two girls, twelve or thirteen years old, stood with their bicycles further along the bank.

'Have you seen a little girl? Fair-haired. Six years old.'

They shook their heads and drew back in alarm. 'We haven't seen anybody,' they responded in chorus and left.

I opened the case on the grass bank. Inside was Cindy, naked, with a nail through her chest, her body smeared with mud. My cry echoed from the opposite bank of the river.

I ran along the gravel path towards the bridge, kicking away a branch lying across the path. Where was everybody? Why was nobody swimming? All sound had vanished: from the river, from the road, silent and dead. I ran as hard as I could towards the bridge and the waterfall and thought I heard her lovely little voice: 'Daddy,' but there was no sight of her.

I rubbed my eyes and raised my hand to shade them from the light. Had I heard her voice, or was it just the sound of a bird? I ran onto the bridge and saw her trotting towards me. My knees felt so week that it was all I could do to keep standing when she jumped up to me.

I hugged her and whispered, 'Where have you been?'

'I just went for a little walk,' she whispered back.

'So where did you go, my love?'

'Across to the other side. I saw something shining there. When I got there I saw a doll stuck between the rocks, but when I got right down I couldn't get back up and I didn't know what to do.'

'Oh dear.'

'The rocks were too big.'

'Mmm.'

'Then the man found me.' She held on tightly round my neck and wouldn't let go.

'Who?'

'The man who helped me, of course.'

I raised my eyes and saw him. He was wearing an overcoat and woollen gloves, with his suit trousers tucked into big, muddy gumboots. He pushed his long white hair aside and looked at me.

'I found her down by the river,' he said.

The faint voice, the skinny smile and the chapped lips. I grew uneasy. 'Is it really you?'

71

He cocked his head to one side, took a wad of tobacco out of his mouth and rolled it into a little ball between his fingers.

'What are you doing here?' I asked.

He laughed. It sounded like a mixture of whistling and whimpering. He blinked pathetically. A doomed wretch, I thought.

'I was sure you were …' I said, putting Emma down.

He smiled shyly. 'Dead?' he whispered. 'That's just a rumour.' He looked down at Emma. 'Is that your daughter, Joe?'

Water from my hair was running down over my face.

'She's lovely.'

'What?'

'She's a very fine little girl.'

The trembling in my diaphragm spread to my legs. 'Stop it.'

He looked across at me, offended. 'Don't you want me to say she's a fine girl?' A deep wrinkle ran across his forehead, as if somebody had tried to cut his head in two. He knelt beside her. 'Anyway, it was nice to meet you.'

Emma nodded to him, smiled and turned back towards me.

'George helped me climb up from the rocks, you know.'

'George?'

'Yes, that's his name.'

I drew Emma towards me and put my hands over her ears. He was still kneeling beside her. 'Where have you been?'

'In prison,' he said, staring at his boots.

Emma pulled my hands away. 'Why? Had you done something bad?'

He cocked his head to one side and looked at her with moist eyes. 'Yes. Something terribly bad, unfortunately.'

He's about to start crying, I thought. The small, unhappy smile on his lips was full of self-pity. Nausea swelled in my throat.

I thought: You'll have to go. You can't stay here. But I couldn't bring myself to move. Something about his face and voice glued me firmly to the bridge.

'I was thirteen years in prison, in Ireland. It was no life at all. Prison breaks you and takes all humanity away from you. When you get out, you are nothing. Do you know what we called it? Bunkersen. There was a special unit for the most dangerous prisoners, the ones who had killed and abused people. Do you know what? They didn't bother about any rules at all in there.' He stood up.

Emma looked at him wide-eyed. 'Is it really like that?'

'Quiet!' I said, lifting her again and holding her close.

'Can't you just go away again?'

He gave a pained smile that I wanted to wipe off his face.

'I've only just come back.' We stood and faced each other, but I couldn't bring myself to speak. 'Have you ever been in prison, Joe? Nobody wants to go back inside. I've served my sentence, Joe, I'm a better person now.'

'Better at what? At telling lies?'

Emma looked anxious.

George looked at her. 'I saw your Dad on TV. I didn't know he wrote books. You and your Mum must be proud of him. Did you know that we were friends once upon a time? We drew pictures together and made up stories. I've read his latest book, couldn't put it down.'

'We have to go,' I said, turning back towards the bridge. My legs were numb, but somehow I began to run.

Behind us I heard his voice as if he was shouting to us through a megaphone, 'Did you know that I've started writing too?'

I ran back to the bathing place.

George called after me, 'I must show you!'

I gathered up our things: the towels, the dolls and Emma's case and took the dolls' pram under my arm. As we walked across the bridge, I looked out for him but I couldn't see him anywhere. On the hill up to our house I stopped and bent double.

'Daddy?' Emma leaned down over me as my stomach churned. 'Daddy, what is it?'

I knelt by the edge of the road, but all that came out was thick, green slime. I crawled between the bushes, my stomach retching.

'Are you sick?'

I felt her little hand on my back as I knelt there, bent double over the blob of mucus which lay on the ground like a squashed earthworm.

'Are you alright?'

I tried to smile. 'Forgot to eat,' I whispered.

'Then we'll go home, OK?' She dried my tears with the palms of her hands.

I nodded.

'Even my Daddy needs to eat and drink,' she said as she helped me up.

Back at the house I called Jenny and left a message to ring back on her answering machine. I thought about the chest in the woods and George's mud-spattered gumboots. What the hell was he doing here? It's not a coincidence. He's not home on holiday. Does he know something about the murder? Is that why he's come back? Has he been trying to tell me what he knows? Was that why he called after me?

We had tomato soup with macaroni for lunch. When I was sick on the way home she had seemed so calm, but as soon as we entered the kitchen it seemed she was overcome by dark thoughts. Now she had gone quiet. She fished the bits of macaroni out of the soup with her spoon, staring at them before lifting the spoon to her mouth.

I smiled at her, my reassuring Daddy smile.

'Do you know him?' she asked in a voice from deep down.

'Who?'

'The man on the bridge. George.'

'You needn't be scared.' I poured a little milk into her soup.

She gave me a firm look. 'I'm not scared.'

'Good.'

'Do you know him?'

I put a little bread into my mouth.

Why had I believed his mother when she had told me he was dead? In Ireland, she had said. He died in Ireland. I had met her at the post office, quite unexpectedly. Hadn't seen her for years. Hadn't thought about George for years. And there she was. Greta Nymann, just like her old self. *How's George getting on?* Her face changed, her lips tightened like an ugly scar across her face. *He died*, she said. *In Ireland.*

'I knew him, my love,' I said to Emma in a reassuring voice, 'when I was a boy.'

'Why was he in prison?'

'I don't know. Now eat up before it gets cold.'

She looked doubtfully at the pale soup. 'He said that he'd killed somebody.'

'That's not what he said.' I ate a little bread and drank some water.

'What did he say then?'

'That there was somebody in the prison who had done that.'

We stared at each other over the table. My tummy rumbled.

'Are you still feeling sick?'

'No, no. It's better now.'

'I think he's killed somebody. Are you upset?'

Imagining Katinka's face I shook my head, unable to say anything.

'He said he'd seen you on TV. He liked your book, Daddy, did you hear that?'

I got up and cleared the table. 'Can't we talk about something else?'

'No!' she screamed.

I turned round sharply. There were tears in her eyes. I lifted and held her, trembling.

75

'I don't want to talk about anything else,' she sobbed.

I stroked her back. 'There, there, my girl. Take it easy.'

She buried her head in my arms.

There was something I had forgotten to ask. 'Did he do anything to you?'

She laid her head on my shoulder and I cuddled her even closer, her warm little forehead against my shoulder.

'Did he do anything with you, down there, by the river?' She didn't say anything and I grasped her face between my hands. 'Emma?'

She nodded, blinked and rubbed her eyes.

'It's important for you to answer me and tell me exactly what happened down there. Do you understand?'

'Nothing happened,' she said. There was something she wasn't telling me.

'Are you sure?' She was quiet again. 'Quite sure?'

'It was just … Something he said.'

'What was that, then?'

She opened and closed her mouth, unable to make a decision.

'What was it then, dear?'

She pushed her head against my chest again. 'I don't understand,' she whimpered.

'Just tell me what he said.' I stroked her hair. 'You can whisper it.'

After a moment I felt her lips against my ear.

'He said that he had once found a tongue lying in the grass.'

'A tongue?'

'It was from a little girl of his, he said.'

I cuddled her close, wondering what Agnes would say when she heard. Not good. Not good at all.

'My love …,' I whispered. 'Don't tell anybody about this. You hear. This will be a secret between us.'

She slept for over an hour after lunch, tossing and turning restlessly, and murmuring sleepily about her best friend, Vera Linn.

I shook as I tried to make telephone contact with Jenny.

The tongue lying in the grass. A little girl cut to pieces.

There was something about the way she said it, the childish way she constructed the sentence that convinced me it was something George really could have said. He wanted to frighten Emma and to frighten me, and to make me think that he had killed Katinka.

The mobile on the kitchen bench started ringing. For God's sake, relax, I thought to myself as it slid across the bench like a slippery bar of soap. It was Jenny.

'Has something happened?' she asked.

'I met somebody, down at Stilla. I think it might be important.'

'OK,' she said distractedly.

'An old friend …,' I began.

'Wait a little, Joe.' Her voice disappeared. 'Joe? I'll need to ring you back.' She hung up.

Damn!

I went in to Emma. She was lying in bed looking up at the paper seagull which twirled round and round under the high ceiling.

'Did you sleep a little?' I sat on the edge of her bed.

'I dreamt that you had two heads,' she said without a smile.

I stroked her cheek. 'Dreams are strange sometimes.'

She nodded. 'Shall we go back to Mummy again?'

'Yes.'

We drove slowly along the road to Solemskogen through a light drizzle of rain.

Agnes's father's house was at the edge of the woods, a low-lying, modernist house with large windowpanes and natural colour pinewood panels. He had designed it himself ten years before, and I sensed that he wanted to create a building which discreetly underlined the thinking man's harmony with nature.

The only effect it ever had on me was to give me a slight headache.

As I turned in towards the terrace, a splash from a muddy pothole hit the windscreen. Through the dirty glass, the house and the garden looked mucky and alien. I got out of the car into the rain. Agnes stood on the step, looking good in her red jeans. Behind her, the spruce woods stretched towards the fields and the ski-tracks and the lakes. It seemed to me that the forest was devouring the little house. I walked over to the natural stone step. Her eyes looked dead. All hope is gone, I thought. We can never be a couple again.

I tried to smile.

'My God, you look terrible,' Agnes said quietly. 'Has something happened?'

I shook my head and looked down at her bare feet and then up to her wet hair. She'd just had a shower. Had she been out running? Or had a visitor? A man, perhaps? Good God. I stroked my face, as if to wipe away these twisted thoughts, and looked her straight in the face. A direct, deliberate look.

'We met somebody ...,' I began. My voice cracked.

Emma was still sitting in the car, fumbling with something in her little case.

Agnes looked at me, obviously worried. 'Who?'

'Down by the river. Emma ... wandered off.'

'What? What are you trying to say?'

'Nothing dangerous happened, but it was awkward.'

'For God's sake, what are you trying to tell me?'

I thought of George's muddy boots. Couldn't tell her about that. Couldn't say anything about George until I had spoken to Jenny. It would have frightened her out of her wits.

'I was asleep, down there.'

'At Stilla?'

'Yes. When I wakened she had gone.'

'Are you making a fool of me?'

'I dropped off for a few minutes.'

78

'Damn you, Joe!'

'I'm sorry. I didn't mean to. I didn't sleep at all last night.'

'I don't care a damn about that.'

'I understand.'

'Where was she, then?'

'She had gone for a little walk, by herself.'

'A walk?'

'Along the river.'

She bent forwards towards me. 'If you do that again, I'll kill you.'

Emma came wandering across the lawn with her case in her hand. She stopped and looked at me. 'Are you still upset, Daddy?'

'No.' I shook my head. 'I'm fine now, but you must tell Mummy what happened to Cindy.'

Emma put the case down on the step and opened it.

'Cindy got a nail through her tummy, and then she was dead.' Her eyes sparkled with a grim enthusiasm as she held Cindy up in front of us. 'She was buried in the case and sent out to sea.'

Agnes quickly shifted her gaze towards me. 'Did you see any of this?'

I shook my head. 'I didn't see any of it. I was asleep. When I wakened …'

'But she came back to life again,' said Emma, and now she's fine, just like before.' She looked at us with a little grown-up look and handed Cindy to Agnes.

Agnes looked at the disfigured, soiled little blonde figure with the hole in her belly. 'Dear God,' she murmured. 'She's lucky to be alive.'

11

Driving down towards Kjelsas, I felt as overwhelmed as a ditch full of dirty water and eventually stopped by the edge of the road in Lachmanns Way. I called Jenny again, but got her answering machine. 'Call me back, for God's sake!' I shouted. 'Didn't you want to take a statement from me? I've got a lot to say.'

When I got home, I looked out the DVD of the TV interview the Chief Editor gave me. I needed to check what I had actually said about George. The Book Programme logo came up onscreen.

The studio was set up like an interview room, with two chairs and a small plastic table in the middle, and a microphone on the table beside a jug of water and two glasses. A one way window on the long wall gave the impression that an investigator on the other side was mercilessly gauging me.

The presenter, Siri Greaker, had red hair. She was younger than I imagined; twenty-eight or twenty-nine with a round face and a shower of pale freckles that gave her a reassuring, childlike appearance. When she smiled, she developed an amazingly deep, hollow wrinkle in her left cheek.

'This year Joe Uddermann has published a novel which is both disturbing and shocking,' she said. 'A novel about children with black souls.'

I looked pale.

'Welcome, Joe.'

'Thank you.' My smile looked more like a nervous twitch.

'Can you tell me about what you have committed?'

'Committed?'

'Yes ... to the page.'

'It's an autobiographical novel. I grew up in Brekke in the north side of Oslo. Some people call it Frysja, after the ancient name for the Aker River. It's a fairly typical Oslo district with a mixture of buildings, industry, terraced houses, detached houses, blocks of flats. It lies along the river, near paths and fields which are good for walking and jogging. I went to Kelsas School.'

I shut my eyes and remembered the school which had burnt down, opened them and looked at myself again. The camera moved to show the interviewer and interviewee from above. A lamp reflected off the one-way window.

'In third year ...' I babbled on, incoherent and nervous, suddenly stopping to grab the glass of water and empty it with one gulp.

'In third year a new boy joined our class. His name was George. That first day he seemed like he would just blend into the crowd and disappear. He was wearing a light blue shirt buttoned right up to his neck, a Jean-Paul jacket and yachting shoes. Typical early nineties style.'

Siri Greaker gave a slight laugh and nodded encouragingly.

'But when I looked at him again, there was something not right, something sad and *dead* about him, as if he had experienced something terrible. It sounds strange, but that made me really curious. I wanted to really know that guy'

'You've called your book *The Chalk*. Why is that?'

'They called George *The Chalk* because he had such white hair.'

'How did you become friends?'

'Every day after school I walked home through a wood. I found him there one day, lying on the ground, moaning. There was blood round his mouth and he had two loose teeth. He told me that two boys from school had beaten him up because of his white hair.'

Siri Greaker blinked in the light from the studio lamps. Her smile had vanished. 'Because of his hair?'

'Yes, and I thought that must be wrong, obviously. I invited him home and after that we began to hang out together. George was good at drawing, really talented. He thought up gloomy stories. We made up our own series.'

'Cartoon series?'

'We wanted to be cartoon designers. We sat in the attic for hours, drawing. George liked to draw accidents, I remember, car crashes with human parts strewn over the road.'

'You too?'

'No, but I enjoyed watching him. It was like watching something come to life.'

'But then one day he set fire to your school.'

I clicked the pause button. The TV picture of my face froze as I sat with my hand on the remote control. If George had seen the programme, if he had a recording of it, he must have sat as I was sitting now, spooling back and forward, trying to work out what I was thinking. Perhaps his heart would have thudded in his chest and perhaps – without realising it – he would have clenched his teeth so hard that his jaw ached. While he looked at the picture of my mouth, about to say something about the fire at the school, was he so angry he couldn't stay sitting, and while he continued watching, forcing himself, did he begin to swear, softly at first, inaudibly, a whispered stream of obscene and hateful curses?

I pressed 'play' again, and my mouth, began to speak.

'It could have been a disaster,' I said on the TV screen. 'I remember a girl who was on fire, her clothes burning as she ran through the playground. Two pupils were admitted to hospital with severe burns. The rest of us escaped just with fright. I thought a lot about it afterwards, how narrowly we escaped being burnt inside the building.'

There was total silence in the studio for a few seconds.

'Why did you decide to write this book, after all these years?'

82

'I happened to meet George's mother in the post office a couple of years ago, and asked how he was getting on. I hadn't seen either her or her son for many, many years. She told me that he had died, in Ireland, and that set me thinking about what had happened at that time, back in our childhood.'

'Was it difficult to write about a person you had actually known?'

'Yes, it was difficult,' I said, leaning slightly forward. Then the camera switched to a close up of the author's pale face. 'You can't always trust your memory. I didn't feel confident that my memory was reliable or neutral. The text appeared to be both factual and fictional. A first person narrator seemed to stand out, an "I." Was that really me? Did I believe in this "I" character? Is it possible to believe in someone who writes about himself?'

'Some critics have described your book as a study of a destructive child, a person who could have become a terrorist and gone on to do much greater damage, though what he did was bad enough. Why did he do it?'

Siri Greaker was both demanding and curious.

'It's not easy to give a short answer,' I replied. 'I've devoted almost three hundred pages to it.'

A faint smile crossed her face. I wasn't going to get off the hook. 'Nevertheless, formulate it a little more briefly.'

'There's one thing I can say. I've read a lot about evil, from philosophers, neuroscientists, behavioural psychologists, criminologists. One thing that surprises me is how seldom anyone writes about the *joy* of destruction. A lot has been written about the sociopath's dysfunction, about lack of empathy, non-empathetic personalities and so on. The factors driving personality, hyper-egoism, the "algebra of aggression".

'None of these traits typified George. None of the books I read described anybody like him. I didn't find his personality

83

type in any of the categories. He wasn't devoid of feelings; quite the contrary, he had a sort of hypersensitive and artistic temperament. He *enjoyed* playing the role of the loser and *wanted* to be trodden on. He was unique and wanted to accomplish unique things, great things. Whenever he had the opportunity to tear something down, a light came into his eyes, and when I sat down many years later to figure out why he had done the things he did, the phrase which first came into my head was "destructive joy."'

'Destructive joy?'

I nodded, realising how animated I had become.

'The joy of knocking things down, the feeling you experience as a child when you knock down the Lego tower you spent hours building. All the effort, the toilsome work of setting block upon block and regulating the balance is worth it for the few seconds of ecstasy when you tear it down. It's the same pleasure you get from Barbie dolls by setting fire to their hair, or tearing their arms off or poking their eyes out with a little nail, to see what they look like now with new, damaged eyes.'

Siri Greaker didn't have the faintest idea what I was talking about.

'Do you understand?'

'Yes, yes, it all make sense,' she said. She leaned towards me to hear more.

'Soren Kierkegaard writes somewhere about "lust for destruction". A Swiss-American researcher called Gina Neuberger claims there are gene combinations which act together towards the joy of destruction. The fact is though, nobody can give a precise answer as to why some people are attracted to violence and destruction.'

Siri Greaker thought for a moment. 'Did it worry you; that you didn't understand exactly?'

'I think an event like that is bound to trouble us if we don't discover some answer. I really think we want to search for that answer, no matter how disagreeable and complicated it might be.'

'Was that "joy in destruction" the nearest you came to an answer to who he was?'

'Some people say that wickedness is the opposite of love, but the more I thought about George, the more convinced I became that he had a ruinous talent, a talent for destruction.

'What happened to him?'

After the fire at the school, people said, "He is evil. He has no soul". I didn't know what to believe. I had been his friend and couldn't stop thinking about that.'

'What do you mean?'

'Why did I want to be his friend? What did that say about *me*?

I pressed the pause button again, shut my eyes and realised how worn out I felt, as if something was about to crack apart. I had felt like this before, when I was putting the finishing touches to the novel. I had to stop frequently, to abandon the keyboard and the screen. It was as if all the questions were about to smother me. I had to go out, to try to get rid of the feeling that everything was falling apart.

I walked through the birch woods, down towards the river. As I went, I felt that people were watching me from inside the thickets down at the riverbank. Characters from my novel, the people I was writing about; watching me from between the branches with radiant, expectant faces, waiting for me to fall.

I carried on beside the river. The branches hung out over the surface of the water, their ends tangled together in the shadow of the trees. I hurried past the bathing place and the brick houses, across the bridge and the waterfall and back to the crooked house I had inherited from my father.

Siri Greaker looked at me more insistently, no longer so young and innocent. 'What do you think of your friend now, Joe?'

'It was good that he died,' I blurted back.

I moved close to the TV screen. It looked as if Siri Greaker was about to say something, but no words came. Her lips were chalk white.

'You don't understand,' I said. Something in him had been completely destroyed. So it was good that he died.' I paused. '*I'll burn everything down. Nothing will remain. And then they'll chase me through the streets like a dog.*'

'Pardon?' Siri Greaker seemed confused.

'Nothing,' I said. 'It was something he wrote in one of our cartoon series which suddenly came to mind.'

I switched the TV off, feeling dark and uneasy. 'Satan was in it too,' I whispered, rubbing my eyes hard.

Lying on the sofa I tried to relax, but my chest was tight and I struggled to breathe. I had gone on too long, said too much. I took a deep breath and held it for a moment, let it out slowly through my nose and relaxed.

The text message with the picture of Katinka and me had been taken the evening before she died. Had her killer taken it? Could be. Perhaps he was standing outside my window right now. Maybe he was taking another picture through the living room window. I got up, couldn't let things be, walked to the window, pressed my face against it and looked out. Nobody there. I picked up my cellphone. A new picture message? Of me standing there looking into the garden? No. Not that. No, but that didn't mean he wasn't out there. It didn't mean that he wasn't following my every move. It didn't mean that he wouldn't kill me too and pack my body in a chest. The message had been a warning of punishment.

I was guilty beyond reasonable doubt. I had laid my wife's best friend and written a book about a dead childhood comrade. The sentence had been delivered and was now being served: Agnes had left me; George turned out not to be dead.

The room seemed to shrink and my brain shrivelled like a frightened little animal. Needing to breathe I thumped my

86

chest. Lights flashed in front of my eyes, as if I was on a roller coaster. I cried out and sat up and it was as if a bubble burst in my chest. I could breathe again.

In the bathroom I rinsed my face in ice-cold water, but the phone was ringing insistently in the living room. I dashed through, got hold of it just in time and heard Jenny's solemn voice at the other end. 'I need to talk to you!' I yelled.

'Calm down.'

'I can't bloody well calm down. Somebody's trying to kill me.'

'Why do you think that?'

A twinge of pain in my guts. 'Oh!'

The mobile phone vanished from my hand and slid away across the floor.

Jenny's voice: 'Joe, are you there?'

I picked up the phone again. 'Yes. Sorry.'

'Did you drop the phone?'

'Yes. I need to talk to you.'

'Not now.'

Panic again. Tight throat, unable to breathe. 'Then when? You said you would call me in for an interview.'

'I know. Sorry I haven't called you back.'

'Why didn't you?' She didn't answer. 'When can we talk then?'

'I don't know, Joe. There are a couple of things I need to find out before we have that talk.'

'What do you mean?'

'Don't worry about it. I'll ring you back as soon as I know anything more.' I couldn't say anything to that. 'And, Joe?'

'Yes?'

'Try to relax a little.'

I hung up, gasping for breath.

Nearly midnight, but I knew I wouldn't sleep. I took a pill, washed it down with beer, sat in the dark living room and awaited developments. My eyes scanned back and forth across the windows and out towards the dark garden. I went over and drew the curtains, took *The Chalk* from the bookshelf and started reading from page 48:

'Many years later I met George's mother in the post office. Until that day I had forgotten all about the fire-raiser and his mother, Nina. She was an unusual woman with long, fair hair hanging half way down her back. I took my place beside her in the queue and words rattled out of me, like a rehearsed politeness.

"Hello, Mrs. Nymann!"

She looked at me carefully for a few seconds before she recognised me and said my name.

I nodded and smiled. "How's George?"

There was an awkward pause. "He's dead," she said in a flat voice.

I looked at her pinched face. What? Surely he couldn't be dead.

"He died in Ireland," she added.

"Oh, that's terrible. I'm sorry."

She looked at me as if I was the world's biggest liar and turned towards the barrier. I wanted to grab her by the shoulder and make her look at me, so that I could say ...

What? That I had often thought about him? That I missed him?

It wouldn't have worked out like that. She would have seen through me, and I couldn't have coped with her reaction.

"What was he doing in Ireland?" I asked. "How did it happen?"

She shrugged her shoulders. "Why do you ask?"

I mumbled a sort of apology and stumbled out of the post office. As I walked home, I wondered how I could have forgotten him. My cousin said she thought that everybody had forgotten him. I remembered how he wanted to burn us all and flatten the school to the ground. How could we forget that?

After all the excitement had died down and the shock had turned into a horrible memory, silence descended on the school grounds. We spoke in lowered tones, as if we were embarrassed about something but didn't quite know what.

Had he really gone to this school? Was he one of us? If he really was an *evil child*, why hadn't someone stopped him? Nobody could say anything about that – none of the teachers, none of the pupils. Nobody wanted to talk about him.

The fire was soon forgotten and that autumn he was sent to an institution. I knew that he was out there somewhere, but I was just like the others; I couldn't cope with painful memories. Quite soon, we all forgot him and I forgot that for several months we had been best mates.'

I reckoned that he himself started the rumour that he was dead, asking his mother to tell everyone that he had died in Ireland. He had given her detailed instructions, and she had followed them to the letter.

Say that I'm dead, he had said. In Ireland. Say that I'm buried over there.

I went to bed and read a little from *The Dark Half*: 'You are disturbing the peaceful mood I'm in. You are destroying the frame of mind I'm in. You are disturbing my peaceful frame of mind.'

Then I put the book down and closed my eyes. I wanted to get some sleep.

12

Just before three o'clock I was wakened by a horrible whining noise. I sat up in bed and peered around in the dark at the alarm clock and the lamp on the bedside table and the pattern on the curtains. The noise continued. Opening the curtains I looked out of the window, towards my neighbour's yard. Not a light to be seen. Surely he wouldn't use a drill in the middle of the night?

Now I realised that the noise was coming from inside my own living room. My feet felt like heavy stones as I walked across the floor of the bedroom, opened the door into the living room and, in the dark, saw a green spot of light from the TV on-off switch.

The infernal sound grew louder. Where in hell was it coming from? I wandered back and forth across the living room and into the kitchen. There were no machines in the house which could make a noise like that. I put my hands to my ears and shouted, 'Stop!'

The noise disappeared but as soon as I took my hands away it came back.

Through the chink in the curtains, I looked out into the garden. The branches of the apple trees hung twisted in the darkness of the night. A crow was sitting immobile on one of them.

The sound must be coming from somewhere inside. I opened the fridge and checked the fire alarm, stared at the radio and unscrewed the housing from underneath, unplugged the leads of all the appliances in the house. Then I unscrewed the covers from all the gadgets: the DVD player, the decoder, the telephone connection box, pulled the fridge and the cooker away from the wall and looked under them with a torch. I found nothing and, not knowing what I was looking for anyway, stood exhausted in the living room contemplating the screwdriver in my hand.

Then I swallowed another sleeping pill.

When I woke in the morning I was trembling. It was as if I had been lying in a grave all night, and couldn't remember what I had been dreaming about.

At half past six I got into the car. The radio forecast said low pressure would persist and give rise to further precipitation during the next few days. I turned the radio off and drove along Frysjaveien, past the warehouses and office complexes and the old plywood factory. Raindrops splashed onto the windscreen like big blobs of spit, and a layer of scum built up beyond the range of the windscreen wipers. Streams flowing to the river were full and running hard. Soon it would be overflowing its banks again.

I parked in the basement car park in Nydalen and took the lift to the fourth floor where Jenny lived. She had moved in about a year ago, but her name still wasn't on the door; there was just an empty frame. I stood in front of the peephole and waited for her shadow to appear in the opaque glass panel.

'Hello, cousin,' she greeted me. She had grains of sleep in her eyes but gave me a big hug, and I felt a wave of bodily warmth. 'Isn't it a bit early?'

She was wearing a black dressing gown. For a moment, I thought that she would slam the door in my face and ask me to come back when she had more time. Instead she opened the door fully. 'Can you pick up the paper?'

I picked it up from the doormat and we went into the kitchen. 'You look hellish,' she said.

'Had a bad night.'

'I understand.' She set out two cups. 'What's going on,

91

Joe? Why are you here at the crack of dawn?' She dropped a lump of sugar into her cup and stirred it with a ballpoint pen.

I cleared my throat, thumped my chest. Something was stuck in there. 'I met George, at Stilla,' I said.

She looked at me uncomprehendingly. 'George?'

'George Nymann.'

'*George Nymann?*'

I nodded.

'Have you gone mad?'

I shook my head. 'I took Emma down to Stilla yesterday to go swimming. It's quiet in the mornings. She's getting quite good.'

I took a gulp of coffee. Strong. Picked up a sugar lump and dropped it into the coal-black liquid. 'I fell asleep for a few minutes and, when I woke up, she was gone. After a few minutes she came walking over the bridge with a man. I didn't recognise him at first.'

Jenny shook her head. 'George is dead.'

My hands clasped the coffee cup tightly. For a fleeting moment I imagined it breaking and the coffee spilling all over the table. 'How do you know that?

'That's what you wrote in your book, Joe.'

I shuddered again. 'I know.'

I turned the warm cup round in my hands. I didn't find him in the census record and his mother said he was dead. Perhaps she had a reason for lying. Perhaps someone had asked her to? Have you thought of that?'

Her mouth wrinkled, as it always does when something is bothering her. Not daring to look at her tight expression, I looked down at the floor between my shoes. There was a little reddish brown spot. What the hell was that? Coffee? Blood?

Pull yourself together. You've not slept well. Look up. Don't be scared. You can talk to Jenny. Look her straight in the eyes and try to appear relaxed, indifferent.

92

I looked up. Was that a contemptuous smile on her face?

'Did you speak with him, then?'

'Yes.' I told her what George had said.

Jenny shut her eyes, so that I wouldn't notice her professional detective suspiciousness beginning to engage. 'Ireland?'

I nodded. I had looked at pictures on the internet of the prison which people referred to as *The Bunker*. The high, yellow prison walls. The lighting masts. The towers. The guards. The barbed wire. The cramped cells. There was a picture of a man sitting at a table. The back of his head and neck, tattooed with a flame.

'I'll try to find out what it's all about,' she said, opening her eyes.

'He told me he had started *writing*.' Jenny wrinkled her forehead. 'What are you thinking about?'

'Nothing.'

'I can *see* there's something you're thinking about.' Now I noticed how worried she looked. 'Do you think I've discovered something?'

'I don't know.'

'Don't know?' My voice was too high. *She doesn't care!*

'You'll need to speak to someone else, Joe.'

'What?'

'We are cousins. I can't discuss this case with you any more, at least not here.'

'Then just listen!'

'What?'

I twirled the coffee cup round and round. She looked at me expectantly. 'If you have anything to say, Joe, now is the time to say it.'

'I've got a feeling that something's going to happen to me,' I said, abandoning my unconcerned expression. 'He wants to revenge himself. For the book, maybe. He's come back to… I don't know… drive me mad, perhaps…' I tried to laugh.

93

She wanted to speak, but something stopped her.

'Say something then, Jenny.'

'OK. But then you must promise to go home and wind down. OK?'

I nodded. 'We've arrested somebody.'

'Who?'

'Yesterday we got some pictures from a security camera in a sports shop at Storo Shopping Centre. They show a man who has been convicted for abusing several women standing behind Katinka at the cash desk and following her out. Another camera shows him just a few minutes later driving up Maridalen. She was found the following morning.'

'Does he know her?'

'We don't know. The interview starts in a few hours. I need to have a shower and get going.' She drank the rest of her coffee in one big gulp and went into the bedroom.

I stood up, dizzy, and followed her. 'The murderer knew her.'

'How do you know that?'

'I just know.'

She turned round towards me in the doorway to the bedroom, which was in darkness. Her voice was determined. 'You really must go now, Joe.' I didn't budge. 'I'll get somebody to investigate George Nymann, I promise, but now you must go home.' She wrote a telephone number on a post-it note and handed it to me. 'Here's a colleague you can speak to if anything happens.'

I swallowed. 'How does that help me?'

'It's all I can do.'

'There's so much more I should have told you.' My voice cracked.

'Go home and try to get some sleep. You've had a lot to cope with in the past few days.'

A wave of anger came over me, and for the first time I felt

an urge to shove her. 'I hadn't expected this of you,' I said as I hurried out of the flat.

The door slammed behind me with a dull thud.

Jenny's worried look haunted me as I ran down the steps to the basement car park. Did she think I had lost my grip?'

Something was wrong. Both front doors were wide open. I looked around carefully in case someone was standing behind a concrete wall with an iron pipe in his hand. When I reached the car and leant down to look inside he would strike. The iron bar would split my skull in two. It would go quiet. Dark. Then I would hear the sound of an ambulance in the distance.

The only sound I could hear was my own breathing. The stereo was still there. Nothing had been removed. There were no surprises on the seats.

You're not in a film ... it's not a game ... nobody is after you ...

I bent down and looked on the back seat. There was nothing unusual to be seen. I got up, closed my eyes for three seconds, waited for the iron bar, but there was no swishing sound.

Maybe I forgot to lock the car. Some school kids could have noticed a door open and sat inside for a laugh. I started the engine, and backed out of the parking space.

No, I hadn't lost my grip. Nobody had come to kill me, and nobody was following me and trying to drive me mad. Jenny would continue her investigations. The police would solve the case. Everything would at last be as clear as water. Was that right, I thought, clear as *water*? Is that the right phrase? I opened the window to get some air. The sound of the building's air conditioning was like the roar of a river as I drove out of the car park.

As I drove up Maridalsveien the rain became heavier.

What a hellish early summer! Frysjaveien was running with muddy water which sprayed up from the wheels. A man in a rain cape ran fearfully across the road. I glanced up at the sky. Wasn't it about time the rain stopped?

As I drove the car into the garage a shadow flitted across the wall. Was there somebody there, behind the stack of winter tyres, a man with a blood stained spade in his hand?

No! Stop … look around you, man. Nobody here, nobody at all behind the stack of tyres. It's just your brain playing tricks with you.

Laughing slightly at myself, I pulled my jacket over my head and ran up the gravel path towards the house. In the dense rain I didn't see the dog until I was nearly at the door. Its paws were sticking out between the apple trees and there were red spots in the grass. The skinny beast was lying with its forepaws stretched forwards, as if at the moment of death it had stretched in a last impossible attempt to escape from the man with the spade. Its mouth was full of dried blood.

September, 1990

13

Walking home along the path which wound through the trees I stopped to listen to the crows cawing in the treetops. Invisible up there in the canopy, they sounded as if they were being strangled. My mother did say that I was a dreamer. The cawing faded and disappeared and I heard a different noise, in a clump of bushes; not birds. I shoved the branches aside.

He was lying there hiding, with the Jean Paul jacket over his head. I crawled under the bush and whispered his name, 'George?'

He pulled the jacket tighter, mumbled something and cowered on the ground. I got a grip on the arm of the jacket and pulled. He clung on determinedly, but eventually whimpered and let go. His mouth and cheeks were smeared with blood.

'What's happened?' He said nothing. 'Has someone hit you?'

I looked at his bloody teeth. Things like that don't happen here, not at our school. The boys here were mostly OK. I'd never seen anyone beaten on the way home from school before, and I'd never seen anyone get their teeth kicked in.

'George? What's happened?'

He said they had held him down and I looked at his tear-filled eyes.

'Who?'

'The boys in third year. They kicked me in the mouth,' he squeaked softly.

I couldn't stop looking at his loose teeth, wobbling to and fro.

'It's because of my hair.' Blood ran from his lips as he spoke. 'They say it's ugly. It was just because of my hair. That's why they held me down and kicked me. They said they didn't want to see monsters like me at school.'

My parents were out so we went home to my house where he could wash in the bathroom. I threw away the bloody towel and we went up to the attic where I often played undisturbed under the roof beams. A spot of blood had clotted in his hair.

'Why do you think they hate people with white hair?' he whispered.

I had never heard of any such thing, a hatred of white hair. I opened a skylight so we could look at the crows fluttering round the chimney. I fetched a bundle of comic papers. 'They'll have forgotten about it by tomorrow,' I said. 'About your hair.'

He looked at me sadly. It didn't look as if he thought they would give up.

'You should tell the teacher.'

He shook his head and picked up an old *Donald Duck* comic, browsing a little before putting it down. 'You must never tell anybody about this,' he said seriously. 'That would make it much worse for me.'

'Worse for you?'

He nodded. 'They said they would poke my eyes out.'

I shivered and was speechless, imagining his eyes being poked out with a knife. I didn't want to think about it.

George wondered if I had something we could draw on. I fetched a box of coloured pencils and a big block of paper. He spent several minutes bending over the pencil box, picking the pencils up one by one, looking at them and putting them back. Finally he chose a black and a yellow. A little squint smile grew across his lips and he used the two pencils to draw the face of a girl.

I laughed. 'Who's that?'

He looked up at me. A shaft of light fell from the skylight on his eyes. He blinked. 'Can't you see?'

I bent down for a closer look. He had drawn her slanting eyes perfectly. Her hair was darker though. 'It's difficult to draw dark brown hair,' he said.

'It's Katinka,' I replied.

His eyes shone. 'She sits beside me in class.'

I couldn't help laughing. 'Do you like her?'

He blushed. 'Maybe just a little.'

'Everybody likes Katinka.'

'Everybody? Why is that?'

'I don't know. They say she's the prettiest girl in the class.'

'*The prettiest girl in the class.* No wonder everybody likes her.'

I laughed and he began to laugh too, the oddest laugh I had ever heard. 'Maybe she's in love with you?'

We doubled up with laughter, two skinny nerds, one with thick glasses and a squint and the other with chalk-white hair. Neither of us stood a chance with Katinka.

'Maybe she does love me!'

'Yes!'

We grew quiet, and he went on drawing.

The next day, I spotted him on the road between Kjelsas School and the train station, motionless with his back to me. I called, but when he turned he appeared not to recognise me.

'Hi, George.'

He blinked and turned away again.

'What are you looking for,' I asked, trying not to seem too inquisitive.

He stared towards the parking place and the station. 'My mum,' he whispered. 'She's supposed to be coming to fetch me.'

I had heard that he lived with his mother in an old shack in Maridalen, but I thought maybe that was just a rumour. We watched until an old van drove into the parking place and stopped at the grassy slope where we were standing. A long toot of the horn sounded.

'That's her,' he mumbled without moving.

A seagull circled the station and flew towards the Technical Museum.

'Shouldn't you go down to her?'

'Yes,' he said, but he didn't move.

Two girls walked hand in hand across the parking place, their satchels dangling from side to side. One of them turned to look at the van, Katinka. I turned towards George, and saw that it was she he was watching.

'Can I come home with you?' I asked on a sudden impulse.

'What?'

His face looked so sad, even though he smiled. I thought he would say no, that I couldn't, but he put his hand on my shoulder and we walked together towards the parking place, like old comrades. His breath seemed to be rising and falling with a slight wheeze, and I wondered if perhaps he had a chill or maybe asthma or bronchitis.

Katinka glanced over her shoulder towards us several times. When she smiled I felt excited, but wondered if she was laughing at us. As we approached the van, George let go of my shoulder and climbed into the back seat.

'Hello, Love,' his mother greeted him, without taking her eye off the railway station and the girls who were now looking towards the van. Katinka leaned towards Agnes and whispered something to her, and then they laughed and ran towards the bathing place.

George's mother started the motor and I got in and settled into the seat, which felt cold against my back. She had white hair which hung down over her shoulders. It wasn't just fair or blonde, but completely white like a piece of paper, and I thought it looked good after a fashion. She was wearing a formal jacket, such as stylish old men wear on National Day on 17th May. Her shirt was buttoned to the neck, with a fold of skin protruding over the edge of the collar. She reversed the van out from the parking space.

'How was your day, then?' she asked without turning round.

102

When George didn't answer she glanced in the mirror and noticed me.

'Hello, I didn't see you. That's nice, you've brought a little friend with you, George.'

George looked at me too. 'I don't think he's so little.'

'What's he called then,' she asked.

'Joe.'

'Joe?'

'Yes, that's his name.'

'Hi, I'm Greta,' she said politely. 'Are you coming home with us?'

I nodded. 'If I may?'

She laughed and drove out of the parking place. 'We've just recently moved to the town, Joe. We've lived in England since George was little, but there weren't any ...'

'What?'

'Children. Where we lived.'

'Oh?'

'He's not used to having friends,' Greta explained. George stared through the window and said nothing. 'That was why he had to play alone while I was working at the theatre.'

George stared out of the window. 'Can we talk about something else?'

I looked at Greta's face in the mirror. She was pretty, but not in the way other women are pretty. Her face was long and narrow, and her eyes shone. She lowered her voice. 'He's a little shy.'

We were driving beside the water, but it was hidden by trees crowding like black streaks into the very edge of the road. Past the trees we could see over the glittering lake.

'Mum's an actor,' George said, staring out of the window. 'Or was an actor. Now she's writing a book.'

'A book?'

'About a woman who leaves her husband and her child to go and live out in the woods,' George explained.

103

I looked at Greta's face from the side. She smiled, but didn't appear to be listening to what he said.

'She likes the woods better than people.'

Greta asked, 'Do you read, Joe?'

I shrugged my shoulders. 'Mostly comic strips.'

George asked, 'Why can't you write a book about me, Mum?'

George was looking at the back of his mother's head. He had said more to her than I had ever heard him say before.

'What would it be about, George?' she asked.

'About me.'

'Do you think that would be an interesting book?'

'At any rate I'm much more interesting than the damned woods.' Greta smiled at him in the mirror, but her eyes were serious. 'I'm going to be somebody special,' he said.

'You always say that.'

'But it's true. You can't recognise it. Just wait and see. I'm going to …'

'What?'

'Be famous.'

'Oh yes?'

'Yes.'

'Then I'll write a book about you, my boy. I promise.'

George looked at her furiously. 'Don't you think I'd like to write the book myself?'

Greta just laughed. 'Yes, maybe that would be best, but what are you going to be famous for?'

'Wait and see.'

'Yes, yes,' she said softly. 'That'll really be exciting.'

George had clenched his fists, and his knuckles were white. I looked out over the lake at the little waves rippling across the surface.

'OK, Joe?' I nodded. 'You look pale. Are you car-sick?'

'Just a little.'

'Oh, that's a shame.'

'I'll be alright,' I whispered.

She turned and looked at me with concern. 'We can make pancakes when we get home. I've bought eggs, and blueberry jam. Do you like pancakes with blueberry jam, Joe?'

'Yes.'

'That's fine.'

George turned towards the window again and we drove to Maridalen in silence.

A gravel road wound through the dense forest and for a while I thought that Greta had taken a wrong turning, or that the old house by the waterside didn't exist at all and the whole thing was a story or a misunderstanding. The trees overshadowed the road, wrapping the car in forest gloom, but then light shone through the treetops and a dark little lake appeared before us. At the head of the bay stood a small wooden house with a grassy clearing in front. Two big oaks cast a shadow over the door.

'This is where we live. Isn't it lovely?' Greta scrambled out of the van. 'I love the peace and quiet beside the water. Isn't it charming?'

Paint was scaling off the walls and lying like little patches of skin on the grass. The windows were cracked and the chimney-pipe was askew.

'She likes old shacks,' George explained. 'Anything that's old.'

'Not really,' Greta corrected him. 'I like things with soul.'

I didn't understand, but agreed that the house was special. The fading paint on the walls and little dark windows made it look like an old face. I followed George down steep steps to a basement.

The walls of his room were lined with coarse brown fabric and there was a faint scent of resin. On the floor was a Persian rug with a tear in it and, hanging from the ceiling, a light fitment with two flickering bulbs. A picture of a massive explosion hung on the wall over George's bed.

105

'What's that?'

'The atom bomb which fell over Hiroshima in 1945.' We knelt on his bed and studied the picture. 'I got it from our neighbour in England. An old chap. I think he was a hundred, or at least ninety-nine. He had been in the bomber. During the war.' He pointed to the big cloud in the picture.

'The temperature in the town rose to four thousand degrees. In just a few seconds people and buildings and animals were turned to dust. Altogether eight hundred and twenty thousand people were killed.'

'That's terrible!'

'They were fried in the amazing heat. Their skin curled and their eyes fell out and the bodies shrivelled to half their size in a few seconds.'

'How do you know so much about that?'

He looked at me in amazement. 'I read everything I can about the War.'

I felt sick, and wondered whether Greta had forgotten about the pancakes. George was still looking at the picture, as if he couldn't take his eyes off it. 'Do you think we'll get the pancakes?'

'What?'

'The pancakes and blueberry jam.'

George looked up at the ceiling. 'That was just something she said.' I heard Indian music from the kitchen overhead. 'Do you hear it?' he asked.

I listened. George pointed at the ceiling. 'She's meditating. We mustn't disturb her.' He took out a packet of biscuits and gave it to me. There was a big pad of drawing paper on the table.

'Can I look at it?' I asked.

George smiled.

I opened the pad. Every sheet had a drawing of a girl.

'Who's that?'

'Girls.'

I turned over the page. Eyes, lips, delicate ears, hair. 'Who is it? I don't understand.'

'Don't you see?'

Then I understood and began to laugh. 'They're the same girl.'

'Yes.' He smiled a little.

'Katinka.' I thought of Katinka turning towards us at the parking place. Had they spoken to each other? Was there something going on?

George opened the box of 'Kandahar' pencils and began drawing on the last sheet in the pad.

'When it's finished I'll give it to her.' He smiled secretively.

A week later the drawing was ready.

'What do you think?'

We were sitting in his basement room again. He had proudly taken the sheet out from the pad. I looked at it for a long time before I could say anything.

'Don't you like it?'

It was incredibly good. The first picture of her he had drawn at my house was nothing beside it. It was as if Katinka was staring at me from the sheet, and I felt a strange stirring in my guts. I swallowed 'It's brilliant.'

As I cycled home, I couldn't stop thinking about the picture and about what Katinka would say when she got it. When I went to bed that evening, I could see her face in front of me and had to open my eyes to check that she wasn't there.

I liked his picture, but I didn't want her to like it as much as she liked me.

Everybody at school could see that the picture was good. One day he went up to her at break and handed it to her, rolled up carefully and tied with a piece of string.

'What on Earth is that?' she asked, glancing at the giggling girls around her.

'It's for you. A present.'

'A present? Why are you giving me a *present*?'

'Because you're beautiful.'

The girls laughed and clapped their hands and yelled. Katinka held her hand up in the air and they were all quiet. 'Don't laugh,' she said. 'It was beautifully spoken. Let's see …' The girls clustered round her. 'A present … because I'm beautiful …'

She looked as if she was pleased and thought it was fun, but when she unrolled the picture it was as if she had seen a ghost. What was she thinking? Why did her smile vanish? She looked frightened.

Rolling up the picture again she threw it on the ground. When she looked at George, her eyes were angry. 'Bloody whitehead!' she hissed, trod on the picture and ran off.

All the other girls looked at George as if he had spat on her, and ran after her to console her. They didn't bother to look at his picture again.

George stood motionless, with a tense smile on his lips. He seemed not to have heard what she said, or noticed her throwing the picture to the ground and treading on it.

Through the years I often wondered why she was so angry.

While I was writing the book about George and the fire at the school and my childhood, I realised that I needed to talk to Katinka, to know what she thought about the drawing. I needed to find out what she really thought of George.

I hadn't seen her for many years until I met her again in the café and thought that she looked incredibly well. She had lived her whole life without showing any signs of wear. Her skin was naturally glossy, and her teeth were white. The parties and setbacks and disappointments and the fear that she was throwing away her life on a God-forsaken farm in Telemark had bounced off. She still looked as she had at sixteen – as ravishingly beautiful as when she left Frysja 'to find herself'.

'Why were you so angry about that picture?'

She laughed. I watched her mouth timidly, like a fourteen year old, and remembered what it had been like to kiss those lips which still looked exactly as they had in the light of a paraffin lamp in a hut in the woods more than twenty years before.

'Good God, Joe, that was a hundred years ago.'

'Surely you remember the drawing he made of you?'

The only thing she remembered was that he fascinated her. 'Maybe I was a little bit in love.'

'Were you? With *him*?'

'Yes, maybe …'

'But he was …'

'Small and strange. I know. Maybe that was why. Maybe that's why I was interested in you too.'

'Because I was an ugly little nerd with thick glasses?'

'That, perhaps. You were the undertaker's son, and George was the white haired little gnome from Maridalen. You were like two cartoon characters, the pair of you.'

When she laughed I couldn't take my eyes off the gap between her front teeth.

'Two cartoon characters …' I laughed too.

'But he was even uglier than you,' she said, 'and that obviously made him more interesting.'

'You're just saying that.'

She shook her head. 'He sent shivers up my spine.'

'Really?'

'Yes. He really was spooky. And a little bit exciting. I think I didn't dare to admit it, didn't want to show anybody that I was interested in a boy like that. I was pretty and popular right from when we went to primary school. Wasn't I?'

'Yes, of course.' I wanted to say that she still was, but held back.

'The picture really was fantastic, but I think I felt embarrassed that he had drawn me, even though I liked it.'

That's what she told me, many years later.

109

14

We ran across the school yard and unlocked our bikes under the birch tree in Asbjornsensvei. Behind the brick walls and dark windows the school bell was still ringing. We looked at each other over the handlebars and made the secret sign that George had invented before speeding away, leaving the other pupils to stroll across the yard with all the time in the world. We didn't have all the time in the world. We wanted to be gone as quickly as possible.

George had the red Tomahawk with chopper handlebars and a small front wheel that his mother gave to him when they moved to Norway. I had a blue Diamond with eight gears. We raced each other along the winding roads in Maridalen, where the swirl of yellow dust clung to our legs. I glanced across at George and for a moment we just looked at each other.

Greta was out walking in the woods as usual, and we had the house to ourselves. We drank juice and ate biscuits and read comics: *The Phantom; The Hulk; Sprint.*

One of the comics we read several times was *The Guest*, about a boy who had been in a coma after an accident. One night he woke up in hospital and didn't know where he was. A nurse spoke to him, but he didn't understand what she was saying. They tried sign language and showed him pictures, but he didn't understand a thing. He was thinking in a different language, but didn't know what it was or whether anybody else understood. One night he ran away and went into a big town and watched the trains, the cars, people hurrying homewards. He didn't recognise anything. It was all just strange, meaningless shapes and he felt threatened. He crept under a bridge and began to plan how he could revenge himself and destroy as much as possible of what he saw.

We often drew. I watched George, following his pencil strokes as he sat bowed over the pages. Precise and accurate, he had lots of ideas for stories although some were sick. Drawings of children chopped to bits. People without hands and feet. Feet sewn onto arms. Hands sewn onto feet. People trying to walk with hands as feet and feet as hands. Faces which had been cut to pieces. Burnt. People tied to big wheels. Fingers which had been cut off. Children with stab holes in their bellies.

He had drawn a whole book full of sick drawings.

He was bent over the paper, really concentrating. When he finished he showed me the result with exultation in his face, except that he didn't smile. He looked proud, as if he had drawn a plan for a city. One day I found him sitting in the shadow of the school wall, rummaging in his satchel.

'What's wrong?' I walked over to him as the school bell stopped ringing. He looked down in his satchel as if he had seen a snake.

'My pencils.'

'What?'

'The coloured pencils. My Kandahar pencils.'

'What about them?'

'They've gone. Somebody's stolen them.'

Three nights later we stood in the garden in front of Katinka's house. She lived with her mother in a white painted wooden house in Jetteveien. Her mother was old, grey haired and wrinkled like an apple in autumn. She didn't look at all like her daughter; it was difficult to believe that they were related. Katinka was tall and pretty, with a tough, cheeky expression. Her mother was short, with a frightened look and a low voice, and she enjoyed working in the garden. The flowerbeds in front of the house bloomed, and Virginia creeper climbed up the walls.

From our stance among the rose bushes we looked up at Katinka's open bedroom window. A blood vessel thumped in my throat, and I regretted agreeing to come on this expedition.

George had said that we must meet at twelve o'clock; it was important. I had climbed out of my bedroom window, jumped onto the grass and crept away shortly before twelve. The blood vessel had been thumping in my throat all that time. George was waiting for me behind the garage at Katinka's house. Pointing to the window he told me we were going to steal the pencils back.

'Are you sure it's Katinka who stole them?'

George whispered, '*Surely you know that.*'

I nodded, not daring to contradict him.

We took our shoes off and sneaked across the lawn. I grabbed his arm and pointed to the kitchen window. There was a light on but it seemed there was nobody there.

George grasped the downpipe and started climbing. My legs felt numb. Halfway up the wall he turned and looked down at me and whispered, '*Wait there.*'

He crawled inside and then it was quiet. I stared up and wondered what he was doing. How long would he go on searching?

I started climbing up the pipe, and whispered his name, '*George?*' I looked down, and caught the scent of the bed of night phlox.

A tap was turned on in the house. I paused, my arms feeling as if they were being pulled out of their sockets, before climbing further, as quietly as I could, and hoisting myself through the window. I knelt down.

On the wall above me were posters of pop stars and a

112

shelf of old dolls, on the desk a huge cactus with long spikes. Katinka lay with her face towards me, sleeping with her mouth open. Her eyelids twitched. The bedcover was decorated with plump little angels blowing trumpets but where the hell was George?

In the bed beside her! He had closed his eyes, but was smiling in his 'sleep.'

'*George?*' I crept over to the bed.

He had sneaked into the bed between her body and the edge, and was lying beside her secretly in the dark, his face close to hers.

'*George?*'

I ducked down, as quick as lightning, and looked up into Katinka's blue eyes. She saw me in her sleep and closed them again, sighed and rolled over. George slid out of the bed and stood beside her, looking at me with a secretive smile and the box of coloured pencils in his hands.

Where had he found them?

He shoved the pencil-box under his jacket and bent over the bed again.

'*What the hell are you doing?*' I nodded towards the bed.

He was looking at her carefully, as if he was studying a drawing. He leaned towards me and whispered, '*I don't think she's really that pretty.*'

We both looked at her, the light from the window on her face. I swallowed, my chest felt tight.

'*Shall we set fire to her?*'

'*What?*'

He was holding a matchbox. He lit a match and held it towards the bed and her lovely face.

I grabbed it from him and stamped it out and he smiled an angry smile.

Katinka didn't move.

When we got back to the garden he turned his back to me.

'George,' I said, gripping him by the arm. He pulled himself

113

free and walked towards the bicycles. I followed. 'What the hell ...'

'Must go home,' he mumbled, jumping onto his bike.

'Were you really going to set fire to her?'

He was already well away down the road. I wakened that night thinking my bed was on fire.

George wasn't at school the next day. Somebody said he was ill. I walked with Vebjorn on the way home. Vebjorn had a constant smile, but a strange and solemn gleam in his eyes. He was in his third year at that time. After we had been walking for a while he said, 'Is it true that you're hanging out with George?'

I shrugged my shoulders. Everybody knew that Vebjorn was a gossip, and I had no wish to tell him anything. 'Sometimes.'

'You really want to?'

I looked at his round face and narrowed eyes. 'What do you mean?'

'You know that he fakes it?'

'Fakes it?'

'Didn't you know? He just makes it up.'

'What are you going on about?'

'Wasn't it you that found him in the woods, when he said that some boys in third year had beaten him up?' Vebjorn chuckled and made a strange grimace. 'It's just lies. He's acting.'

'I don't believe you.'

'Nobody has touched a hair of his ugly little head. Everybody knows that, you idiot.'

He crossed the road, towards Sagdammen, and I ran after him. I didn't believe a word, but nevertheless wanted to hear more. 'So tell me what you know.'

Vebjorn smacked his lips as if he was sucking on a sweet. 'He's trying to get people to feel sorry for him, but it's not genuine. He kicked a stone on the ground. 'He's sly.'

'I saw it with my own eyes, Vebjorn,' I said. 'He had blood on his teeth.'

'Oh yeah? Do you know what he did?'

'No.'

'He banged his head on the wall until the skin broke. I was standing just a few metres from him, on the other side of the fence. His forehead was bleeding. It was a real cut. Blood ran down into his eyes. He didn't think anybody had seen him. Then he walked along the corridor so everybody could see and knocked on the rector's door. And he snivelled like anything.'

'You liar!' I yelled.

Vebjorn screwed up his eyes. 'Ask the rector.'

We stopped on the other side of the bridge and the dam. The waterfall roared in the background. I felt a cold shiver, not knowing what to believe.

'Don't you realise how sick he is?' Vebjorn said mockingly. He turned and went home.

That evening I lay in bed staring at the ceiling, at a shadow drifting back and forth that I couldn't stop watching. It was as if a light had been lit inside my forehead and, when I shut my eyes, I saw the fine drawing George had made of Katinka.

15

I sat alone in a corner of the yard one day when George wasn't at school. I could have cycled over to see him, but didn't. Ever since we met I had thought there was something strange about him. I wanted to be his friend, but was scared. Had he really found his coloured pencils in Katinka's room, or was that just a dramatic pretence? Was what Vebjorn said true? Was George a liar? Would he lie to me? Was I a liar too when I yelled at Vebjorn that he, Vebjorn, was lying? Why would I want to be friends with a liar and a thief? Totally absorbed in these thoughts I saw George beside Katinka in the bed. Hosts of little angels with trumpets were swirling round his head, the matchstick, a bed on fire.

'Do you know that guy, the Chalk?' Katinka was bending over me and I was startled by her hoarse, girlish voice. My mother had said she had a twinkle in her eye, and that had fascinated me. Her face was only a few centimetres from mine, lighting up my little dark corner. I savoured the scent of her breath.

'May I?' She sat beside me. She was wearing a sleeveless T-shirt which showed her long, milk-white arms and the little mole on her right shoulder. 'Is it OK for me to sit here?'

I nodded. 'Yes, of course.'

She leaned across and asked secretively, 'Is it true that he's in love with me? She had three freckles under her left eye. I hesitated and looked around. Was anybody watching? Was she teasing?

She was so lovely I could hardly bear looking at her. It

116

was as if I had been enveloped in an unbearably thick and fantastically delicious mist which made breathing painful.

Over the next few weeks, Katinka and I talked a lot together during break-times, sitting in the darkest corner of the shed. She seemed to like me, but I didn't understand why. I wasn't popular. I was ugly and skinny, had glasses and a squint, and my hair was straggly. One day I asked, 'Wouldn't you rather hang out with your girl friends?'

She cocked her head to one side and answered, 'I like hanging out with you.'

'But I'm just...'

She laughed and ruffled my hair. That's what's good about you, Joe, you're not conceited.'

She glanced contemptuously at the gang of boys by the fence. Some people called them hooligans, but they weren't really so bad. They generally left me in peace.

Perhaps something had happened, I thought, something had persuaded her to distance herself from the 'hooligans' and hang out with a cartoon nerd like me. Then again, I wasn't dangerous. She could flirt a little. I wasn't conceited, because I knew for sure that she just wanted me for a friend, that she and I could never be lovers. Then one day on the way home from school she said something amazing. It's different with you, Joe.'

I blushed at the mere thought that it could be 'different' with an ugly little chap like me. When I realised I was smiling, even though I didn't want to show it, I asked, 'What do you mean?'

'The other boys,' she said, 'they're so boring.'

My head was buzzing. She was so lovely to look at, it was if she shone. I closed my eyes and walked on silently, enclosed in a madly delightful haze.

Katinka. Katinka.

What did she mean? I lay thinking about her at night.

Katinka, the finest girl in the class. Why did she think I was less 'boring?' I didn't understand, but I was tingling all over.

Every time I visualised her face, it was as if I caught the scent from her mouth and her neck and her cheeks, and my heart thumped so hard that it hurt.

We chummed each other on the way home from school almost every day of that October. The trees by the riverbank were yellow and red. We stopped on the bridge and looked down at the river, watching leaves and twigs and sediment rushing towards the waterfall, our hands side by side on the railing. I pointed to a black rubbish bag bobbing in the water. As I put my hand back onto the handrail, I touched her fingers and it felt as if I had stuck my hand into an oven. I drew back and looked at my fingers as if they were burnt. Katinka laughed and asked if I would go home with her.

'I'd love to.'

We walked for a while without saying anything and I could see that she was thinking about something, but didn't want to ask. When we came to the garage in front of her house, she stopped and put both arms around my neck. It felt as if she was clinging to me, it was so hard to breathe. 'Will you come with me on a trip to the hut?'

'What?' I stumbled back against the garage door. She didn't let go, just laughed and followed me and explained that the family had an old hut in Maridalen that she sometimes got permission to borrow for a visit with some girlfriends.

I didn't understand. Would I go on a trip to the hut with a crowd of girls?

'No. It will just be the two of us,' she said.

I took a deep breath. *Keep calm.*

I had never stayed in a hut with a girl. *Just the two of us.* That was scary. What would we *do*? Katinka laughed. I think she saw what I was thinking, for she said that it was just a completely ordinary trip to the hut. I shrugged my shoulders and tried to laugh too, but I think it must have sounded odd, because she ruffled my hair and said, 'Relax, Joe. We'll just talk and be happy, as usual. It's just a walk in the woods, nothing more than that.'

I nodded and thought that I should relax, that it didn't mean anything more than that we were going to stay at the hut, but my legs trembled as I walked home. I was in a daze, and when I opened the door at home I felt as if I was a different person.

I told my mother that one of the boys in my class had invited me to his family's hut. She smiled and said that was alright. I think she was glad that I had found new friends other than George. She asked if he would be there.

'Don't you like him?' She shrugged her shoulders. 'Have you something against him?'

'I don't know.' She gave me with that now-we-must-have-a-little-talk-together look which I felt was becoming rather tiresome. I had no wish to talk and nothing to say. 'He's a *strange* boy,' she said thoughtfully. 'What is it about him?'

'Nothing.'

'Nothing? Don't you think there *is* something?'

'What exactly?'

'I don't know. Can't quite put my finger on it. There's something about his mood?'

'*His mood?*'

'Hmm,' she said, suddenly looking sad. I don't know. I … Just forget it.'

'Yes.'

She smiled. She was waiting for me to tell her more, but I didn't know what I should say.

'Anyway, he's not going to be there.'

'That's alright then.'

'So can I go?'

'Sure you can. Just be careful.'

'About what?'

'I don't know. About everything.'

119

I nodded.

'OK, then. Thanks.'

The following evening I packed a rucksack and lay awake for several hours. As soon as I closed my eyes, I saw Katinka lying asleep while I crawled towards her bed. She opened her eyes, and looked at me. Did she remember that or not?

We arranged to meet on Saturday morning beside the dam at the Oset Reservoir. I stood waiting, wondering from which direction she would come and what she would be wearing. The mist lay like a veil on the water. A bat flew low over the surface, snapping up insects. I heard her bicycle bell before I caught sight of her.

'Hi, Joe!' she called. She was wearing an orange fleece and high-laced mountain boots. We cycled from Langsetlokka towards Sander farm and further on up the valley. Little birds were flitting around the dense rushes at the water's edge.

We were hot and sweaty, and the dust from the gravel road swirled up between our bikes. We drank water from a stream. A man cycled past at full speed. I had to use a stick to prod a cow standing in the middle of the road and Katinka laughed as it ran off. When we arrived at the hut, I had the feeling that I had been there hundreds of times before.

It was built of brown stained timber. The windows were small, with loose panes, and there was a tread missing from the steps. A rusty horseshoe hung on a nail above a broad door and a chopping block stood on the ground in front of a decrepit woodshed. A big birch tree with yellow leaves leaned over the roof.

'You look as if you've seen a ghost,' she said, holding her hand to the sunlight.

'I feel as if I've been here before,' I said, looking around the clearing.

'You are funny,' she said, as she clasped my face in her hands and kissed me.

120

A warm glow spread round my mouth. 'What are you doing?'

'Kiss me, you scarecrow.'

'What?'

She put her face right up against mine and bit my lip.

I backed off. 'Ouch.'

She did it again. 'Kiss me then, go on!'

I held her tightly and kissed her. Not having kissed a girl before I didn't know how to do it.

I carefully pushed my tongue inside her mouth and felt the cold tip of hers against mine as it moved in my mouth. She closed her eyes and pressed her breasts against my chest. She pushed me away, laughing. 'That's that,' she said, and went into the hut.

After the kissing we behaved like an old couple, as if we had known each other for many years. We prepared food. We washed the kitchen bench and lit candles and the paraffin lamp and played cards at the dining table; crazy eights and rummy. She put on one of her mother's old tapes, The Kinks: 'Something Else,' 'Waterloo Sunset.' We laughed at the music and she danced a little while I watched and quite forgot that she had kissed me.

We lit the stove and sat on a sheepskin rug on the floor, talked about school and parents and everything. In the middle of the little room stood a wooden table and some chairs. Above the old wood-burning stove, a shotgun and a photograph of a man hunting hung from a nail. A wrought iron candelabra hung from the ceiling. I lay on my back and let my eye roam around the old objects in the hut: the paraffin lamps, the check curtains at the windows, the simple wooden table, and the stove with the shotgun above it and the picture of the hunter.

'Is that your Dad?'

Katinka looked up. 'That's Granddad,' she said, my Mum's dad. He disappeared in the mountains.'

'Disappeared?'

121

'He went out hunting and never came back.'

'Sad.'

By eleven o'clock we were getting tired. She gave me a hug and we undressed and each went to our own bed.

I bade her goodnight, as a grown man says goodnight to his dearest after a long, happy day. I felt relaxed and sleepy, and fell asleep as soon as I shut my eyes.

During the night I heard noises. Was it a branch scraping against the roof? I went back to sleep, but wakened again and thought I heard a door being opened.

I got up and looked in the lobby. All was dark in the hut, but there was a torch lying on the floor. I switched it on. Katinka's bedroom was on the other side of the kitchen. Somebody was sitting on the edge of her bed, and a whimpering sound coming from under the bedclothes. I shone the light onto his face. George smiled and turned his head to look at me.

'Hi, Joe.'

'What are you doing here?'

'I just happened to be passing, Joe.' His pathetic smile persisted.

'What the hell do you mean?'

'I saw your bike by the hut. So I came in. We're still friends, aren't we?'

Katinka looked pleadingly at me over the edge of the duvet. 'Please,' she whispered, 'get him away from me.'

George looked down at her. His smile vanished. He shook his head seriously, spread his hands and enquired, 'What's up with her, Joe? Is she a whore?'

I looked at Katinka. Tears were running down over her cheeks. 'He had his hands under the duvet.'

'What?'

George spread his hands again, pretending innocence.

I looked at the duvet and imagined his little hands creeping under it, towards her warm, sleeping flesh and in between her thighs.

'I was just curious.'

Katinka's eyes were red.

George was still smiling innocently. 'I just wanted to know about her.'

Without realising it, I had lifted the torch above my head. Now I could see that he was looking at it with a contented expression on his face, as if he knew what was about to happen and, above all else, wanted to happen. It hit him right above the eye, and he slid down from the bed. Pitch darkness engulfed the room.

'Go away!' Katinka screamed.

He crawled away across the floor. I ran after him, sat on his back and pressed his face against the floor. 'What were you doing in there, George?'

His face was close against mine. 'Red,' he whispered.

'What?'

'Her hair, down there,' he said proudly. 'Deep red.' His eyes gleamed.

'You're sick.'

'You know what that means, don't you?' I didn't want to know. 'It means bad luck.'

'Shut up!' I told him.

'Do something, Joe.' His teeth flashed. 'Go on, hit me or something.'

Katinka came out of the bedroom. She had put on a dressing gown.

'Go on,' he persisted. 'Kick me. Hit me!' We looked at each other, Katinka and I. 'Set me on fire or something.'

Katinka walked across, pushed a rug aside and opened the trap door to the cellar. 'Throw him down there,' she said, pointing at the hole in the ground.

A rickety stair ran steeply down. I took a grip of George's jacket and lifted him up from the floor. A stench of wet earth and dead mice wafted up from the cellar.

He spat in my face. 'Say something then, you ugly monster!'

123

I threw him down the stair, surprised at how easy it was, like throwing a match onto a bonfire. Katinka shut the trap door and replaced the rug. We stood for a while listening to the faint whimpering from under the floor.

'He can stay there till morning,' she said.

I could hear him whispering my name from under the trap door. *'Joe, are you there? I'm sorry, Joe. I didn't mean it. Please. Don't leave me down here. I'm scared. Let me out, Joe. Please. I'll never bother you again.'*

I went into Katinka's room and sat down on the edge of the bed beside her. She had lit a paraffin lamp. 'You're strong,' she said.

I looked at her in the lamplight. 'Do you think he hurt himself when he fell?' I imagined what it would look like down there in the earthen cellar: old potato crates and rotting planks and piles of roofing slates covered in spiders' webs. An old toolbox in the middle of the floor, a roll of tape, a rusty hammer, with a rusty axe lying beside it.

'I don't give a damn,' she replied.

I sat closer to her. 'Maybe he fell on an axe.'

'Yes.' I felt her breath on my face. 'Maybe it split his head in two,' she laughed.

I nodded. My cheek rubbed against hers, and I put my hand on her bare knee.

'He deserves to die,' she said.

I felt her sweet breath on my face again. She took my hand and placed it on her breast. She opened her mouth. I put my mouth to hers and felt the cool tip of her tongue against mine, like a little snake.

I shut my eyes and all was dark. I didn't think about George lying in the cellar and maybe bleeding from a cut on his head. I clasped her breasts again and she put her hand on my thigh. We lay back on the bed and my hand slid down over her naked belly, over her navel and the crest of her hip, and right down to where I could feel the red hairs against my fingertips.

I couldn't sleep any more that night. I lay with my face against her back and listened to her deep, slow, breathing, but my head felt as if it was lit by a powerful light from within.

Eventually I slipped out and opened the trapdoor to the cellar. 'George,' I whispered, but there was no reply.

I lit a candle and crept down into the cellar with its rotting wooden crates and dirty beer bottles and mousetraps. At the end of the cellar was an opening just big enough for a boy to crawl through.

Nothing was the same after that. George wasn't at school. Katinka avoided me. She began to walk to and from school with Agnes. She wouldn't look at me, and when I spoke to her she answered with a mumble.

I took a fever and stomach ache and stayed off school for over a week. I hallucinated about George and Katinka. Their faces merged into each other, the beautiful and the ugly, the real and the false smiles, their lips whispering things I didn't understand.

When I came back to school, George was still off. He came back two days later, but kept his distance. He didn't speak to anybody. He had a sticking plaster on his forehead.

The following day, the teacher asked me to remain behind in the classroom after the bell had rung for break. 'Do you know what's happened to George,' he asked.

'George? Why do you ask?'

'I'm a little worried about him. He won't talk to me at all. I just wondered if you knew anything.'

I shook my head.

'The two of you have been together quite a lot, haven't you?'

I nodded.

'Can you maybe try to talk to him?'

'OK.'

As I walked through the corridor I wondered what I should say and whether I would manage to say anything at all. I looked for him in the yard, but didn't find him. I searched all through break, but he was nowhere to be found.

16

During the last period of the following day, the teacher told me to go to the Rector's office. Outside, the school yard was covered in withered leaves. It was late October. My seat was by the window, and I had just taken out my notebook and pencil case.

'Joe, the Rector wants to talk to you,' was all she said. I tried to read in her eyes if she was angry, but couldn't see any clue. She waved me out of the classroom. 'We'll start with the grammar,' I heard her say.

The teacher, apparently worried, had asked me to speak to George. He wasn't here now, and I didn't know what had happened or whether she had spoken to him or what he had said and if it was about me, possibly a made-up story about me.

Out in the corridor, I noticed a crack in one of the windows high above the coat-hooks and name labels. My steps became shorter and shorter as I walked along the corridor. I had never been sent to the Rector before. Somebody must have found out what happened at the hut.

There was a smell of fresh paint in the corridor outside her office. I entered to find a solemn, elderly lady with horn-rimmed glasses and rings on her fingers. My mother said she was sixty-three.

'Sit down,' she said hoarsely, not looking up.

'Thank you.'

I sat on the edge of the chair, feet dangling. There was a smell of fresh paint in here too. The walls were pale yellow, as were her fingertips. Cigarette smoke swirled in my eyes. There was nobody in the school yard, as I could see through the window, but in the middle of the yard was a cardboard box.

'Joe!'

I nodded, startled. She said my name again and set her glasses on her nose. 'How are you getting on?' The light sparkled on the lenses of her glasses.

'What?'

'How are things going with you?' She nodded all the time she was speaking, but her voice was sharp and firm. 'Is everything alright at home, Joe?'

'Yes, yes. Everything's fine.'

'Nothing's happened, has it?'

'No.'

She took her glasses off, held them in her hand, sighed and said, 'Well, well.' There was a packet of cigarettes among the clutter on her desk, *Dunhill Lights*. She took one out, lit it with a lighter and, drew the smoke deep into her lungs. 'I've had a worrying report,' she said.

'Who from?'

She tilted her head and looked at me with the look that adults used when they wished me to say more than I wanted to. I knew they sometimes wondered whether I was 'slow on the uptake', but I was doing alright at school. The Rector put her glasses on again, and her eyes appeared huge. Had George told someone what had happened at the hut?

'I've been speaking to Katinka,' she said.

'Katinka? What about?'

'About your trip to the hut.'

I felt that she was looking right into me, right into what I couldn't bring myself to talk or think about, Katinka's hands pulling me onto the bed and my hands on her naked belly.

'Joe?'

The Rector wanted to 'get to the bottom of it.' She wanted

128

me to talk about what had happened that night, about George and what we had done to him, about the torch and the cellar and his whimpering. She held me in her gaze.

I opened my mouth to say something, anything at all, but all that came out was: 'What?'

Could Katinka have told what we did in the bed? About what we did to George? The torch. The blood in his eyes. How he crawled across the floor in the dark. How I ran after him.

He couldn't breathe. He lay down in the cellar, pleading. He had fallen and hurt himself, and he wanted me to let him out. He tried to get up. He had blood in his eyes. He couldn't lift his legs. He was under water. The darkness was running down into his lungs. He was gulping darkness, he couldn't breathe. He was thinking about us in the bed, Katinka kissing me, my hands on her belly.

I felt her pointed tongue in my mouth. She took my hand and led it down between her legs. The fine, smooth hair between her legs. The moisture.

He found the axe in the dark among the blocks of wood. He managed to get up and lift the axe above his head.

'Tell me what's been bothering you lately.' A piece of ash dropped from the rector's cigarette.

'Nothing's bothering me.'

'What has happened between you?'

He strikes the axe as strongly as he can against the wall, and the splinters splash round him.

'Katinka won't say anything either; about what really happened at the hut.' She glanced down at my wet trainers. I had run through a puddle during break. 'We'll need to have a talk with your parents. We can't have rumours like that around the school.'

'What do you mean?' I asked.

'I don't intend to repeat any of it, Joe, but let me put it like this. There are rumours that some of the pupils from

129

this school have carried out illegal activities while staying at a hut. That in itself is not the school's responsibility, because it happened outwith the school grounds and outwith school hours, but when there are rumours circulating about our pupils we have to look into it. Do you understand?'

'I don't know what you mean.'

'Can't you just tell me what happened, so that we can clear this whole affair up?'

'Who is it that's been saying things about me?'

She didn't answer.

'Is it George?'

Her lips were sealed. I remembered what Vebjorn had said about George going to the Rector to blab about things which had never really happened. Perhaps he had gone to the Rector this time too.

'You know quite well that I can't say anything about that, Joe. Wouldn't it be just as well for you tell the truth?' Light slanted in through the window. Why was there a cardboard box in the middle of the yard? 'If you don't answer now, I'll have to speak to your parents.'

On the other side of the yard, a plume of black smoke rose from the gym hall. 'There's smoke,' I said.

'I beg your pardon?'

I stood up and pointed towards the gym hall.

'From over there!'

The rector put her cigarette onto the ashtray and stood up so quickly her chair rolled back and hit the wall.

I went over to the window as a fire alarm started to wail. A boy was running along the path, away from school. I knew who it was, recognised the hair and the padded jacket. 'It's on fire,' I mumbled, as I felt the rector's firm grip on my arm.

When I came out into the yard, there were flames coming out of the windows of the gym hall. Window panes had already smashed, and there were shards of glass across the asphalt surface. A girl ran across the yard, screaming, jacket on fire. She fell, and the janitor threw his coat over her to smother the flames.

I felt as if I was being held down. My feet seemed far distant. I looked along the road, where the boy had been running, and saw his quilted jacket among the branches of a big birch tree. George was sitting in the tree, staring at the school.

In bed that evening I had a vision of his face, of the flames shooting from the gym hall and George looking at the school and the smoke and the girl running across the yard. He was surely hoping that everything would be eaten by the fire and that when the flames died away all that would be left would be ash and embers and crumbling walls.

The police interviewed Greta and George for the whole of the next day before he confessed. A few days later the Rector told us. 'A tragic incident,' she said.

What we all wondered, though, was what would happen to George. All the Rector would say was that he wouldn't be back, but would he be sent to a children's home, an institution? We didn't know, but we understood that he could never come back to our school and be one of us again.

September, 2012

17

A policeman in civilian clothes came to fetch the dead dog. He packed the body into a plastic bag and put it in the back of his Volvo. I asked if he was looking for evidence.

'Evidence of what?' I didn't like his attitude.

'Surely the poor beast was killed,' I said quietly.

He looked at me with the inscrutable self-satisfaction of a man who has excessive faith in his own judgement. If it had been anyone other than Jenny who had given me his phone number I would have sent in a written complaint.

He prodded the blood stained grass carelessly with the toe of his shoe. 'It looks like an accident,' he drawled sleepily.

'An accident? Did a spade just happen to fall from the sky and hit the poor beast as he was about to lap up a little water?'

He looked at me without expression. 'A roof tile,' he said.

'What?'

'The animal was killed by a falling tile,' he repeated, pointing to the roof.

Sure enough, a couple of the tiles had come loose and slid down, but that didn't mean anything except that the roof needed attention.

'Don't you understand?' I said, approaching him. 'Someone is trying to scare me.'

He looked at me without seeing. For one reason or another, my statements and opinions were not worth considering. He looked up at the roof again and muttered, 'We'll look into it.'

'"*Look into it?*" What the hell does that mean? You saw

the animal yourself, lying on the grass here *in my garden*. You've seen the signs of maltreatment with your own eyes. This is not 'a chance accident' with a loose roof tile. Do you know how many odd things have happened to me recently? Surely you can see that this is a threat? Someone is trying to manipulate and break me down. I assume that you are observant enough to conclude that this is suspicious. No? Do you understand what I'm saying? Or is it outside your *job description* to draw intelligent conclusions?'

He walked back to the car, as if he neither saw me nor heard a word. 'Call me,' was all he said, 'if anything else happens ... if you have any more ... scares.'

I watched the stupid pig drive away before going down to the cellar where I sat at my desk and switched on my MacBook. For several minutes I stared at what I had written, but couldn't remember what it was supposed to be. The start of a new book? The text seemed dreamlike and vague. Gazing at the sentences on the screen, I tried to work out what I had meant. It was clearly something autobiographical and personal, something from real life, but it seemed to have been written without coherent thought and now I couldn't remember what relationship it was supposed to have to reality.

Henry Miller once wrote: *We know that life has no meaning, so therefore it must be given one.*

I had come across that sentence while I was writing *The Chalk*, and it became a guideline for me through the year. I sat and thought about it. How to make the meaningless meaningful? Was that what I had tried here, with complete lack of success? To write about an experience which was poor both in content and in coherence? How could I turn the dead dog with its mouth full of blood into a 'meaningful experience?' How could I give Katinka's gruesome death a meaning?

I had tried to write something about this idea in one of

the chapters of *The Chalk*. I took the book from the shelf and leafed through it hastily. What had I written? It was something about finding meaning ... the author's tendency to ponder everything possible, wasn't it ... Browsing faster and faster, more and more irritated, I worried that I couldn't remember what I myself had written and where it was? Damn! It was no more than a few months since I had read the proofs of the book. I eventually found it. What a relief!

I read aloud: *'The author is by definition a person who is more than normally guided by an underlying uncertainty concerning the coherence of existence or whether there exists at all a word which enables us to talk with certainty about such things.'*

Hm.

I put the book back on the shelf.

What had I been thinking about just before I found the dog in the garden? A shadow flitting across the garage wall ... I had thought ... there was somebody in there, and I'd imagined a man with a spade in his hands and a dog lying on the floor.

I felt sick. Was someone tinkering with my thoughts? Or had I glimpsed the animal on the lawn as I was driving past?

It was like a horror story. I scanned down to the bottom shelf and a dozen books by Edgar Alan Poe: poems, novels, essays. In my early twenties I had been crazy about him and read as many of his novels as I could get a hold of. I read a few sentences from *William Wilson* and put the book down again. The letters on the page were just a jumble. I couldn't concentrate. My eyelids were drooping, but when I closed them I saw the dead dog and the smashed teeth. My eyelids closed again, and sleep came sneaking up on me like an assailant in a dark underground car park.

Walking through a garden in the dark, towards a kitchen door, I stopped and took off my shoes, picked the lock, opened the door and entered the house. All the lights had been turned off. A wall clock ticked. I saw my head reflected in a glass door as I crept through the living room. On a desk there was a PC with unrecognisable characters. I opened the keyboard with a little screwdriver and silently smashed the innards to pieces. Then I went into a bedroom. There was a woman in the bed. I walked over to her quietly, bent down over her and looked at her fresh, beautiful face and gentle lips. She opened her eyes and I thought she was going to scream. I was wakened by a ringing sound.

I was sitting on the chair with my face flat on the table. The clock on the shelf was at 16.50. Still drunk with sleep, I clambered up from the basement to find George in the kitchen with a bundle of papers in his hands, his white hair hanging down over his eyes.

'Hi, Joe.'

I tripped on the door sill and scrambled about on the floor.

'Is everything OK, Joe?' He stretched out his hand, but I managed to get up without help.

'How did you get in?'

He laughed apologetically. 'I rang several times, and when nobody answered I walked round the house to see if you were in the garden. It's lovely outside today. I love the Norwegian summer, but surely everybody does. You weren't there. The door was open, so I came in. I didn't mean to intrude. You're not angry, are you?'

'*Angry?*' I glanced through to the living room. The door was open, but I couldn't remember having opened it.

'Did I do wrong, Joe?' A little smile crept across his cheeks. We stood so close that I could smell his foul breath. I nodded at the bundle of papers in his hands.

'What have you got there?' He clutched the papers to his chest. 'A manuscript?'

'Yes. Or …' His face had an expression of shame and

excitement, like a little boy who had broken the rules and been caught in the act.

I grabbed it out of his hands. There was only one letter on the first page: *U*.

'I wondered if you would read it,' he muttered.

'Why should I do that?'

He shrugged his narrow shoulders.

I took a quick look at the front page.

'*U*. Is that the title?'

'I can't write.'

'That says it all.'

'I'm not a proper author, Joe. Not like you. You have real talent. You're an intellectual, a sort of wise man. This is just something I've scribbled down.'

'Shut up!' I yelled.

He bowed his head again, but I think I saw him smiling.

'I'm sorry …'

Pull yourself together. Think. Get him to relax. Don't scare him away. He's sick. Remember that. Sick in the head. A sick heart. Get him to tell you where he lives. You need to know where he lives so that you can ring Jenny and tell her … that … he … perhaps … potentially …

'Sorry … what are you writing about?'

George tightened his lips.

'Sit down,' I said.

George sat on the edge of the chair. His shirt was buttoned to the neck so that it nipped the skin below his Adam's apple. It looked as if he couldn't breathe. When I thought about it, George had always buttoned his shirt like that, right up to the neck. None of the others at school did that.

'Please don't read it now,' he said softly. 'I'm going to die.'

His sad smile gave me a peculiar feeling.

I took two bottles of beer out of the fridge, opened them and put one on the table in front of him and the other on top of his manuscript.

139

'So you'd like me to read it when you're gone?'

'Yes.'

We both knew that I would never read the wretched manuscript or anything else he had written; I would be sick after a few sentences.

'Cheers,' said George, taking a little swig of beer. His eyes rolled heavenward as he swallowed.

'What are you up to these days, George?'

'Oh, a little here and there.'

I leaned forward over the table. 'What do you really want?'

He tore with his fingers at the label on the beer bottle. 'You don't know what it was like in there,' he said. 'In the prison. You get time to think.'

'What about?'

'About things you've done.' He tore the whole label off the bottle, rolled it into a little ball and laid it on the table. 'I decided to become a new man, Joe. It was then I started writing.'

That could have been good for you, I thought. If it was true. I bet his manuscript was full of borrowed sentences, stolen goods taken a little from here and a little from there, then sewn together to fuck up my brain.

'I believe that everybody has a potential,' he said, looking at me again.

'Why do you say that?'

He smiled secretively.

'Your daughter, for example.'

'What about her?'

'She's sweet.'

I stood up rather too quickly, and the chair banged against the wall behind me.

'Don't you talk about her,' I said, picking the chair up again.

He looked at me with a contented expression, his smile growing broader and broader. He would not be one hundred per cent satisfied until I hit him.

'Don't you think she has potential?'

I sat down again. 'My daughter? For what?'

'For whatever. People can be what they want, most of them. Opera singer, or dancer, or swindler.'

'Or animal killer.'

He nodded. 'Many things are possible.'

'Yes, but some people are willing to go farther than others to achieve what they want.'

'That's right, Joe. You're smart. By the way, what has become of your mother? That beautiful, shy woman? What was her name again? Agatha?'

I nodded at the manuscript again. 'What's your story about?'

He looked at the floor. 'Perhaps you are as good at writing as you once were at drawing?'

A worried frown crossed his face. He hated praise. 'It's about a quite ordinary boy who one day does something evil and destructive.' He gave an anguished smile.

I looked at the thin manuscript. It couldn't have been more than fifty pages long. 'So what did he do?'

'You can read that yourself.'

'Did he frighten a little girl out of her wits?'

He shook his head. 'No, no, it's much worse than that.'

I felt dizzy again, grabbed the beer bottle and drank.

'Is it true that she's moved out?' George asked in a sympathetic tone. He leaned forward and laid his skinny hand on my arm. 'If you want to talk about it, just say. Sometimes it's good to "get it off your chest", so to speak. There aren't many people you can talk to, you don't have many really good friends.'

I drew my arm back and stood up. 'Excuse me, I need to go to the toilet.'

George twirled the beer bottle between his fingers.

I was half way out of the kitchen door.

'I remember your mother,' he said. 'She gave me a drink

of juice once when I was waiting for you. You were out, but she didn't know where you were. You should have been back long before and so I waited for you, but you were away for many hours. She said something to me that I still remember. She said, "Joe is not like other children. He lacks an ability."'

I ought to have given that a moment's reflection, but the words came out before I could stop them. 'Which ability was that?'

He imitated her voice. 'He's too much taken up with himself and can't empathise with others.'

Mother's voice. His face.

'That's a lie.'

'Excuse me?' he looked surprised. 'Oh, sorry. And condolences. I'd quite forgotten that they're dead. That was really terrible, what happened. They were on holiday, weren't they? In Kenya, or was it Tanzania? An accident, out on the Savannah. Tragic affair. Your mother always spoke about Africa and said she wanted to go there. She was a fine person. Altogether too good for your father, the cold fish. Sorry, that must have upset you completely. So gruesome, to lose both one's parents like that. It must have ruined something inside you. Was that when you decided to write these books of yours? I think about your mother especially. There was something special about her. Something genuine.'

I nodded and went into the corridor. 'Back in a moment.'

I locked the bathroom door, took out my cellphone and keyed the policeman's number. I would say he's here, come and fetch him, I'll keep him here.

The ringtone sounded five times, and then the answering service. I keyed Jenny's number, but before she could answer I heard the door slam in the corridor. I ran after him, out the door and down the path, stared up and down the road.

Gone. Damn!

A lorry drove slowly along the street, driven by a woman wearing sunglasses.

I drank the rest of the beer before realising how angry I was. I glanced at the manuscript, and a felt a violent aversion to reading it.

He can't empathise with others.

I looked out of the window. The Volvo was standing beside the picket fence. I would drive to Agnes again. I wanted to see them, Emma and Agnes, check that everything was alright. I wanted to see their faces, Agnes's blonde fringe, Emma's mischievous eyes. I would give my daughter a hug and take her for a walk in the woods.

I ought to have felt relieved that the police had found the killer. Maybe my suspicions about George were exaggerated, but I couldn't stop thinking about his babble and what he had said about my writing and my parents and about Emma's *potential*.

I wanted to go for a run and try to shake off the smell of George and the sight of his hands twirling the beer bottle round and round. I changed and looked out my jogging shoes.

In the car, Mozart.

I parked in front of my father-in-law's house at Solemskogen at half past eight. The curtains were drawn in all the windows. Had Agnes put Emma to bed already? I knocked on the door, but there was no sound. I walked round to the back, knocked on the kitchen door and looked through a gap in the curtains. The kitchen was dark, and the chairs were drawn into the table. There was a yellow washing up glove on the table.

'Agnes,' I shouted up to the bedroom window. She would surely have told me if they were going out. 'Are you at home?'

Agnes never travelled anywhere without telling me, but these weren't normal times. When I called her cellphone I got the automatic answer.

At the front of the house a neighbour was standing in the driveway. He was wearing a red tracksuit top and held a

143

cardboard box under his arm. 'They're not at home' he said, eyeing me suspiciously.

'I can see that. Do you know where they've gone?'

He shook his head. 'There was a break-in last night. I think they left this morning. The little girl was so scared.'

'What?'

'The intruder let himself in through the kitchen door.'

'A break-in? While they were in the house?'

'They were asleep in bed. Nobody was harmed,' the neighbour said slowly while he assessed me, deciding whether I was a decent type or not. 'But obviously, it's very frightening,' he added.

'I'm her father,' I explained.

'What?'

'Emma. The girl.'

'Oh.'

I tried to sound calm and collected.

'Did Agnes say anything about where she was going?'

'Not to me,' said the neighbour, strolling up the flagstone path.

'Were the police here?'

He nodded.

I went back to the kitchen door and examined the lock. It looked as if it had been fiddled with.

18

I parked the car at Sandermosen. Mist swirled down over the old station building as I began my run towards Sinober along the familiar stony path through the woods. A train passed along the valley below with a hollow, whistling sound and I remembered once when I was out running with Agnes, before Emma was born, I slipped on a stone and sprained my ankle. Agnes took the shoe off my swollen foot and helped me to a stream to stick my foot into the ice-cold water. For a few seconds I ran with my eyes shut, picturing us beside the brook.

I'd had a vision of the dead dog lying in the garden, and then dreamt that I was breaking into a house by night. Fantasies were becoming reality. I stopped. What was going on inside my head?

Was he manipulating my thoughts? I didn't believe in such telepathic nonsense and there was another explanation, one that all authors recognise. You start thinking like a character in the novel. You come to believe you are that character. You eat like him and start to walk and run and dream like him. You become an actor, playing a role with mannerisms, joys and phobias. You live as this person thinks and feels. You relinquish your own personality and *become* the character.

I ran up the hill until I heard noises in the undergrowth near Katinka's hut. Flashing lights. Something dark between the trunks of the trees.

'Anybody there?' Thea Dalen stepped in front of me, in her leather uniform jacket. She shone her torch into my face.

'What are you doing here?' she frowned. 'Your usual jogging route?' A lock of hair had stuck to her cheek like a maggot. 'Katinka's hut is in there,' she said.

I looked between the trees towards the timber hut.

'What are you thinking about, Joe? Don't you realise how strange this seems?'

Jenny called from over by the hut: 'Thea!'

A squirrel scurried across the path. 'I'd like to speak to Jenny,' I said.

Thea turned and I followed her through the undergrowth.

In the gloom, the cart track which came into the clearing from the opposite side looked like a pencil line across the grass. Jenny stood at the edge, wearing plastic gloves. The hut was still cordoned off.

'What are you doing here, Joe?' Her face was pale, and I could see that something was wrong.

'Out jogging,' I said, kicking an old, rotten tree stump aside.

Behind her was a black rubbish sack. 'Have you found something?' My voice sounded weak even to me.

Jenny shut her eyes tightly, as if to control a bad headache, as I looked down at the sack. There was a metal box or a wooden chest inside, that kind of shape.

'You can't come sneaking around here, Joe,' she said, and then added in a lower tone, 'Why do you make it so difficult for yourself?'

My throat felt tight, as if I had a blockage. I bent down to cough, and glanced over at the rubbish sack. *A little chest with a rotten heart.*

'Are you alright, Joe?' Thea thumped my back.

I straightened up. 'I thought you'd found the culprit?'

Thea and Jenny looked at each other. 'Everyone we've interviewed has been eliminated. We're still looking.'

Hadn't they arrested the man who had followed Katinka from the sports shop at Storo shopping centre? Jenny had seemed so damned sure. Had he been checked out of the case now? No suspect? They're still looking?

'What about …'

'You can't stay here,' Jenny said, firmly. She put her hand on my shoulder to direct me away. 'You'll need to go.' I shoved away her revolting plastic glove. A gust of wind blew through the woods, lifted her hair away from her eyes and ruffled the black sack. *The heart of a damned whore.*

'What about George?'

'No trace of him.'

Thea elaborated. 'Our people have tried to find him. No address, no telephone number. No relatives have seen him. We've confirmed that he served a sentence in Ireland, but we have no information about him over the past year. His mother still maintains that he's dead. Beyond that we have nothing.'

'Why is she lying?'

'Right now we have no grounds to assume that she's lying.'

Hell! I should have followed him.

'Only one person has seen him. That's you.' Thea looked at me as if I was a snake.

'And Emma. She saw him and spoke to him, but I don't know where Agnes and Emma are. Have you heard from Agnes? There's been a break-in at her father's house.'

'A break-in?' Jenny sounded surprised. 'I haven't heard anything about that.' She looked at Thea.

'I was up there,' I explained. 'Spoke to the neighbour, looked through the kitchen door. The lock had been picked. I called you several times.'

'I'm sure someone is dealing with it.' Thea sounded irritated. 'Perhaps Agnes has gone away for a while?'

'She's not answering my calls.'

'Maybe she doesn't want to talk to you?'

'We'll need to get on here, Joe,' said Jenny. She walked over to the sack.

'I'll try to ring Agnes,' Thea said, blocking me from following. I gave up and walked away, turned onto the track and ran on fast, along the winding tracks among the spruce trees. Sometimes it was completely dark under the dense branches, and it felt as if my feet were finding their way automatically.

While I was taking a shower, an image of a heart muscle came into my head. I tried to call Agnes, but got the answering machine again. I called her dad's cellphone, and wondered why I hadn't tried that before. Was it because I wanted to hear her voice, or because I didn't want to hear his? He answered after a few rings, sounding sleepy and hoarse. "Yes?"'

'It's me. Joe.'

'Hi Joe. What do you want?'

I asked about Emma and Agnes, and he told me they were with him, in the hut at Stavern. 'What about the break-in? Are they OK? What happened? Did you see who it was?'

'You don't need to worry,' he said slowly. It sounded like a warning.

'How can I not worry? May I talk to them?'

He assured me that they were safe, nothing had happened. It had just been someone snooping around in the house. 'A tramp, surely.'

Why the hell did he use that word?

A tramp, a tramp.

'Anyway, can I speak to Agnes?' His voice faded and I thought I heard them talking in the background. 'They're asleep.'

He was lying. I was sure Agnes was sitting on the sofa beside him. 'I can hear her voice.'

'What?'

'Her voice. I can hear her in the background.'

'That's the TV,' he replied in the same flat, unhelpful tone.

'Can you ask her to give me a call, please?'

148

'OK, Joe'

I rang off.

Silly old fogey.

I stood in the garden, drinking a bottle of beer. The limbs of the poor old apple trees were bowed down towards the lawn, as if they were too weak to hold themselves up. I looked towards the river and the mist clinging to the trees.

The sunlight faded from Grefsen Hill and darkness crept down over the roofs. The grass felt cold under my feet. Night fell silently over the river and our houses. Standing there watching the light ebb from the sky, I reflected that this whole place, with the houses and the industrial zones and the old waterworks would be plunged into darkness and the street lights and the lights from the motorway and the home computer screens would go off and all would be pleasantly black and silent. Total night.

As soon as I laid my head on the pillow, I realised how tired I was and how much I wanted to sleep, but I knew from experience that was a bad sign. As soon as I started thinking how important it was, sleep became impossible.

I saw a little chest, painted yellow ochre and red and decorated with iron fittings, an exact miniature copy of the chest they had found her in. Jenny wore plastic gloves as she opened it and looked down. Katinka's heart lay like a curled up foetus.

19

The cellphone was ringing. I got up and scrabbled around on the bedroom floor in the dark. Under the bed I saw the light blue glow from the screen. Had it fallen out of a pocket? The clock on the bedside table was at 22.25.

I answered, 'Joe.'

'It's Iben.'

'Iben?' I sat down on the edge of the bed. 'Hi, Iben.'

'Hi.'

I took the phone away from my ear for a quick glance at the display. The number tallied, but why wasn't she saying anything?

'Sorry to call so late,' she said at last. 'Were you in bed?'

'Not quite. I couldn't sleep.'

Iben had edited all my books. We had worked closely on *The Chalk*. She knew more than most about my uncensored fears and desires, despairs and phobias, but we had never spoken very much about my private life. We had discussed how the book functioned as a text, but she really knew very little about me and I knew almost nothing about her.

I assumed that she was single, and almost took it for granted that she lived alone with her books, that literature was the central focus of her life. But was she really like that? Why didn't I know anything about her, and why hadn't I asked her more about her life, what she enjoyed and what the books and authors really meant to her?

She was breathing unusually fast. 'Thank you for the manuscript.'

'The manuscript?' No reply. 'Iben, are you there?'

'I'll need to sit down to read it again.'

They called her the Falcon because she was both a helper and an overseer. Her raptor's eye was always alert to the concept and writing.

'What are you talking about?'

'I'd thought of calling you in the morning, Joe, but maybe that won't do. I mean, now that I've heard about all you're caught up in. It's terrible. But that's exactly why. I mean ... I thought it was important for me to read your text again and that you would like some feedback. Are you sure I shouldn't just call you early tomorrow morning?'

'No. That's fine.'

'It was very unsettling reading,' she said quickly, 'especially because it's presented so clearly as an autobiographical text. You start by saying that this is a true story. Do you really mean that there is no difference between the narrator and the author?'

'A true story?'

'Yes. That's on page three.'

She was speaking so fast that I couldn't get a word in.

'I'll come straight to the point, Joe. Reading it raises some questions. I wonder what effect you want to have on the reader. The description of the attack on that boy is very uncomfortable reading. It's very disturbing to read a text where the author appears so unsympathetic and manipulative ... so destructive and violent. That was difficult. Sure, it can be interesting ... I mean ... to work with aversion and unease, but here I'm beginning to wonder, I mean, whether there has really been a crime, and then the text starts to deal with another issue, don't you think, about a relationship not just between the author and the reader but between the author and the law.'

151

'Which ...'

Iben drew breath and continued before I could complete the sentence.

'Is it really true, what it says here? The issue is raised very starkly, and is not disproved one way or the other. The events you describe are criminal. How do you intend us to relate to the author as a man with violent and obviously uncontrollable impulses? Not only that, a man who is fascinated by violence and defends and praises it. What are you trying to achieve, Joe? What sort of reaction are you trying to elicit? I really wondered about that. I'm not saying that the text is poor, absolutely not. But I began to wonder. Really. I felt I had to call you to ask.'

'Iben, wait.' She stopped for breath. 'What manuscript?' Silence again. 'Iben. What manuscript are you talking about?'

'*U*,' she said tentatively.

I stood up.

'*U*?'

'Yes,' she whispered.

'I haven't sent you any manuscript.'

Silence. Then her voice came back, more faintly. 'There was a manuscript in my in-box, sent from your e-mail address.'

'Where are you?' She was at home. 'I'm coming to see you.'

'Now?'

'Yes.'

She gave me her address and directions. She lived not very far away, in Sagene.

'OK. Come round then. I won't be able to sleep now. I'll make us a cup of tea.'

I already had the car keys in my hand.

I started to search for George's manuscript in the living room, pulling out the books and newspapers from the shelf under the table. No manuscript there. Damn! I couldn't remember where I had put it. When George gave it to me I was firmly resolved that I would never read it, but now

152

I had to find it, I scurried around in the kitchen, opening cupboards and throwing books on the floor. At last I found it in a pile of old newspapers, opened it at random and began to read:

'There is a side of me that nobody knows. After Katinka died, I haven't been able to think about anything else. I need to tell who I really am. I've written an autobiographical novel, but there is another voice hiding in the text. A confused and destructive man.

'My hands are shaking as I write, because I know that he should never have seen the light of day. I call him Mr. Chaos. It will be disturbing and shameful when I must stand responsible as a scapegoat for what *he* has done.

'I'll try to explain.

'The shy, sensitive and ever so thoughtful author is not genuine. Alas! Your sympathy for me will vanish when you read this. But before you throw the text to the floor and spit out the worst swearwords you know, just remember that all I wanted to do was to tell the truth.

'Spinoza wrote: *Those who repent are doubly weak and miserable, but those who cannot even repent are surely doomed.*

'This is probably the last thing I shall write as an author. All I wish is to confess and be condemned and serve my sentence.

'It's too late to change anything. Katinka is dead. The sun is going down behind the treetops. I cut a hole in her with the sharp little knife and stuffed her down into the chest. Then I started the carefully planned and methodical work of setting the blame on someone else.'

I skimmed rapidly through the rest of the manuscript and threw it at the wall. After gathering it up again I keyed Jenny's number. The answering machine, again. 'This is Jenny's telephone. Please leave a message.'

153

'Jenny. He has written something insane about me and sent it to my editor in the publishing house. Do you understand? He's making me out to be somebody else.'

Hell! That sounded like nonsense. 'Sorry,' I added. 'Just give me a call. I'll try to explain.'

I got into the car and drove recklessly fast towards Sagene.

20

Iben lived in a brick house in an alley behind Sagene Church. In the frame above the door there was an inscription: *Good Pastor Rang's House*. Who on earth was Good Pastor Rang? A local celebrity among Christiania's philanthropists? I had never heard of him.

On the stone step was a pair of gumboots, stained brown and covered in moss and thick straw. I really hadn't thought of Iben as an intrepid walker. The nameplate suggested that she lived alone. I hoped she didn't have a dog. Putting my finger on the antique doorbell I listened for footsteps inside, but heard nothing until the door was opened cautiously.

'Oh hi, Joe.'

Entering the cool, dark hall I had a sense of being embraced by the chaste kindness of the late pastor. I looked around at the arched ceiling and a graduation photo of Iben in her twenties which hung – slightly squint, I thought – from a nail in the wall. She was standing outside a big stone building with gothic pillars, probably a university building.

I wanted to ask about it, but she was already on her way into the kitchen, a long room with a single light fitting above an oak table. On the table were four tea lights in coloured glasses.

'I've not been in your house before,' I said. My eyes were restless, moving involuntarily around the room as if every little detail was worth careful study. An exhausting and bad habit which could lead to details entering the brain and growing to abnormal and unmanageable size.

'I'm sure you haven't,' she confirmed.

I took a chair while she set big china cups and a plate of biscuits on the table. The windowsill was laden with thyme, rosemary and coriander, the bookshelf full of cookery books, an enormous dish of fruit and vegetables and a knife block with Japanese knives. It looked as if she enjoyed cooking. I hadn't expected that. She was so slim and anaemic-looking.

She had brewed a big pot of green tea, which she now poured into the cups.

'I feel sick,' I said, putting the manuscript on the table. The nausea increased every time I looked at it.

'This'll help settle you,' she said, shoving the cup towards me. I looked at the light green tea and took a sip.

'Honey?'

'Yes please.' I stirred a big spoonful of heather honey into the tea and drank a little more.

'And ginger?' I took some ginger, and the nausea began to settle.

Where to begin? I looked at Iben uncertainly. How could I explain to her how peculiar I felt, reading a text which pretended to be mine?

What was it that Roberto Bolaño, the Chilean writer, had written? If all literature becomes autobiography, literature will cease to exist and will turn into a sewer of confidences.

A sewer of fake confessions, I thought. Was that what I was smelling now, the stench from the sewer?

'Think of a picture, a portrait,' I said, looking at Iben's grey, pinched face. 'You've had it hanging on the wall in the passageway for years. You glance at it every time you go out of the house. You often walk right past without looking. You hardly notice it's there, but there's something reassuring about it. One morning you stop to look more carefully.'

'A portrait of myself?'

I nodded. 'At first glance it appears as it always has, but something is wrong. The colour of the eyes is different. The

156

wrinkle on the forehead has grown coarser, deeper. The mouth is grotesque. The face is bloated, sickly, and the lips have thickened. It's no longer a portrait of you, not a portrait at all but a grotesque, malicious forgery. As a portrait it is unrecognisable.

Iben frowned over the edge of her teacup.

'Do you understand? Someone is trying to destroy me.'

'The manuscript was sent from your e-mail address,' she said quietly.

'Yes, he was in the house today. The door to the veranda was open. He could have used my laptop, which was in the living room. I don't know. He's trying to infiltrate me, blacken me from inside, like a plague.

'Who?'

'George. The boy in my book.'

She blinked, and drank more tea.

'It must have been difficult for you,' she said, putting her cup down carefully. 'You've had a hard time recently.'

I didn't like the way she said this. 'It's hellish,' I said, trying to smile.

She looked at me as if I was talking in tongues.

'I'm sorry that you've got mixed up in this.'

'That's not your fault, Joe.'

'No, of course not.'

She didn't seem to understand what she had been reading. I put my hand on the manuscript. 'I don't know if you understand.'

She looked at me quizzically.

'In this insane text I am the perpetrator and he is the victim. Can you imagine how sick and disturbed that is? He writes about how *he* is exposed to *my* criminal misdeeds. It's an infernal fiction, twisted, cut into pieces and stirred together into an unrecognisable, ugly mess.'

'Is it really?'

'He's a cunning little demon.'

Iben drew back a little. She held the teacup defensively in front of her and I realised that I had raised my voice.

'It's typical of him, I should have foreseen it,' I said more quietly. 'He uses his weakness as a weapon. He looks so thin and unhappy, but I don't feel sorry for him.'

Iben pinched the skin on the bridge of her nose. She had been troubled by migraine in the past few years. All that reading had taken its toll.

'He writes as if he were you?'

'Yes.'

'But why?'

She pinched harder and peered at me with an expression I had seen before, when we discussed a chapter she had doubts about. I felt I was in the dock and had to prove my innocence.

'Maybe he wants to get me to behave suspiciously. Maybe that's his plan, to get me to appear as rotten as he is. Maybe he has sent it to others in the publishing house? To other authors? The Society of Authors? The Book Programme? He wants to create confusion. He enjoys that. There's something wrong with him. I should never have written that book. I was sure he was dead, but I still shouldn't have written it. I should have smashed his skull instead.'

Iben put her teacup down.

I realised at once how unbalanced I had sounded. My chest felt tight and my breath caught in my throat. I leaned back to draw breath. 'Sorry. I'm tired.'

Iben surprised me by putting her hand on mine. I hadn't thought of her as one who would stroke an author's hand. I looked down at her little, wrinkled hand. 'It's your style of writing. He must have read your book thoroughly.'

It was hard to breathe. The tea lights flickered in the coloured glasses on the table, sending a bewildering play of shadows onto the wall behind her.

'But Iben ..., I would never have written anything like that. How can it resemble my style when I could never have written it?'

'No, you're obviously right.'

158

I stood unsteadily and picked up the manuscript. 'Don't tell anybody about this,' I mumbled.

Iben stood up too. 'What do you mean?'

'That you mustn't tell anybody I've been here. Don't tell anybody about the manuscript, and that you have read it.'

'Why not?'

I gathered the papers together and tucked them inside my jacket.

'It could be dangerous.'

'For me?' Iben followed me out into the passage. 'What do you mean?'

I turned towards her in the dark entrance hall. She looked scared. 'I'll need to speak to my cousin Jenny, in the police. Maybe she can ... I don't know ... reassure me. But please don't speak to anybody. Lock the doors. I'll call you tomorrow.'

'*Lock the doors?*'

'I'm sorry. I didn't mean to frighten you.' I opened the outer door and walked out into the dark. 'Just lock the doors.'

21

George must have read my book many times, I thought as I drove past Sagene Church. At the side of the building a beggar sat hunched on the footpath close to a take-away food kiosk. George must have made a careful analysis of my syntax, style, typical metaphors and metonyms, use of commas and punctuation, idiosyncratic phrases. He must have read some pages again and again, as if he was terrified of forgetting the text.

Glancing down at the manuscript on the passenger seat beside me, I suddenly realised that the title *U* stood for Uddermann. I stopped the car in Treschowsgata and wondered why I hadn't thought of that before, it was so bloody obvious. Was it because I didn't dare face the implications of his interest? A lorry's headlights flashed across my windscreen. Of course it's humiliating when somebody has such a sick obsession about *you*, and it inevitably draws attention. There surely must be a reason why the person uses nearly all his time and energy thinking and writing about you. Maybe that unfathomable reason was why I had refused to recognise that the title *U* was an abbreviation of my surname.

Hell! I switched off the engine and leant my forehead on the steering wheel. I could see the look in George's face as he read my book. He was sitting in a car, reading in the faint light of the inside lamp. It was dark outside, dark as at the foot of the steep banks of the Aker. He reclined the seat. I did the same, and in my mind saw the cover of *The Chalk*.

He read until his eyes wandered and the letters on the page

160

slid into each other. When he closed his eyes he still saw the description of his own mannerisms: the way he buttoned his shirt right to the neck; his eyes and how he blinked; the constant fiddling of his fingers.

Sitting in the dark, George imagined what the boy in the book looked like. That's me, he thought. It was a compelling portrait, as if the text was more real than his life history, the clear words on the page replacing his confused past.

George fell asleep in the car and woke with the light on his face, picked up the book and read on. It was like an evil child. He loved it and hated it, spat on the pages and then dried them, wept when he read the chapter about the trip to the hut.

Devils from Hell!

Everyone misunderstood him. When he sat on the edge of Katinka's bed, they thought he was going to rape her.

He was innocent but the Devils from Hell were constantly looking for an opportunity to inscribe 'sick murderer' on his forehead. They were so cowardly, and the girl who accused him of raping her was the most cowardly and vicious of them all. He had moved away from her when she started shouting again. He really just wanted to feel her skin, but then that shit of a false friend came running in with the torch and hit him on the head, trying to blind him. For what? For sitting on the edge of her bed and holding her hand? Just because maybe he was a little bit in love with her. They thought his white hair gave them a reason to abuse and humiliate him. They thought that he wouldn't think of revenge.

I opened my eyes and thought: Stop! It's no good carrying on like this. Starting the car I drove up Treschowsgata. I had a long wait at a set of traffic lights which seemed to have got stuck on red. A tight feeling in my chest. My eyes wandered again, I was so damned tired.

*

161

Darkness all round. Warm, really warm. I got up from the bed. I was in a cell. There was something wrong with the central heating system. The heat rose from the floor like red damp. I couldn't breathe. From the neighbouring cell, somebody shouted something in Irish which I didn't understand. Then a different sound filtered into the cell, the sound of fingers on a keyboard, an evil clicking. It was somebody writing about me. The sounds were like little knives stabbing into my skin, my neck, my eyes, my mouth, between my teeth, cutting me to pieces.

I woke with a start to find myself still at the lights. Traffic was speeding along Grefsenveien towards the Storo flyover. Two red buses drove slowly along, one following the other. It was very early morning. I looked around. A young man with a pushchair smiled at me. Did I look odd? The cellphone was on the seat beside me. I had slept there all night, but felt as if I had only nodded off for a few minutes. I stretched. My neck was stiff and sore, but I was breathing more easily and the tight feeling in my chest had gone.

I drove back towards the town centre and the police station.

22

At the reception desk in the police station, I asked for Jenny Uddermann. The duty officer scrutinised me thoroughly and asked in a surprisingly sharp tone, 'Who are you?'

I told him my name.

'Joe Uddermann,' he repeated. 'Just a moment.' He disappeared behind a panel to pick up a phone and I watched the small, jerky, nervous movements of his lips through the glass. *A Mr. Uddermann.* He glanced at me and I looked back at him.

I thought about what Jenny had said about not being able to discuss this case with me, and wondered if there was anybody at all I could speak to. Certainly not the forbidding duty officer.

He was listening carefully. Was Jenny not willing to speak to me? Did she think that I was involved in such a way that she couldn't discuss it with me without compromising her detached and objective professionalism?

The policeman returned. 'Just take a seat and wait a few minutes.'

I sat down, stretched my legs and looked down at my stiff, sore feet. A broken torch rolled across the floor of the hut.

I had always been calm and caring, but I was furious when I hit him in the face with the torch, cut his head and flung him into the cellar. I'm not really like that. He wanted me to smash the torch between his eyes. That was what he had planned.

On the row of chairs facing me, a grey-haired man sat with his arms folded, shaking his head. When he caught sight of me he leaned forward to speak.

'Have you been unlucky too?'

'What?'

'I've lost everything. My hut burned to the ground. All that's left is ashes.' There was something childlike in his gloomy despair. 'It's not the end of the world,' he whispered, shaking his head again.

I looked down at his gumboots, which were covered in grey ash.

Thea Dalen fetched me from reception. She was wearing a dark blue, polo-neck sweater and had split new Nike trainers on her feet.

'Where's Jenny?'

'If you come with me into my office, Joe, we can have a little talk.'

Have a little talk?

I followed her bright new trainers up the stairs.

Inside, the office looked like a cardboard box, but alarmingly bare and tidy, with dull grey walls. On the desk were a laptop computer and a cellphone. That was all. There was a chair in one corner. I sat down.

'Is this your office?' I asked.

Thea sat and looked at the computer screen with inscrutable calm. Her arrogance had irritated me the first time I met her, and in the course of the investigation my impression of her as a manipulator had been reinforced. Strongly reinforced. Several seconds passed before she looked at me again.

'I beg your pardon?'

'Nothing. I just … forget it.'

It was obviously not coincidence that it was Thea rather than Jenny who had fetched me. There were things Thea was planning to ask me about, questions which Jenny couldn't

164

ask because we were family and perhaps also because Thea wanted to question me alone.

'Joe,' she said, before a pause which I understood would not to be followed by a reassurance such as: 'Nothing to worry about, this is just to eliminate you from the case and check that we have all the information we need.' Instead there followed a painful silence, a forced smile, a manipulative grimace.

'Why did you say my name in that tone?'

She laughed. 'In what tone?'

I wanted to say: The cheerful tone which tries to sound so jovial and welcoming but which is really disrespectful and humiliating; but I kept my mouth shut.

"Did I say your name?'

I nodded.

'Alright. I just want to ask you some questions, Joe, concerning Katinka.'

She had said my name again with the same prolonged vowel, as if there was something implicitly ridiculous about it ... Jooooooe.

'I want to speak to Jenny.'

'Jenny can't discuss this case with you.'

Thea had dark stress lines under her eyes. The crease in her forehead had grown deeper and broader, but it was her tone which maddened me, the ingratiating, suspicious, unassailable tone which was apparently polite but which, on careful listening, was full of reproach and scorn.

'If you're not willing to talk to me now, I'll need to call you in for formal questioning.' She folded her arms and smiled.

'Questioning?' I smiled back. 'I'm happy to cooperate.'

Her smile was almost unbearable but I resolved not to let her see so much as a hint of the irritation I felt. I would deny her that pleasure. These are trivia, I thought, nothing important. I rested my hands on my knees and clasped my kneecaps.

'You and Katinka?'

I cleared my throat and nodded solemnly. 'Yes?'

'You had a relationship?'

Her innocent expression looked dangerous. She wanted to persuade me that I had nothing to worry about, but at the same time she knew that I knew that she didn't ask that question without reason. She must already have interviewed a great many people about Katinka and charted her background with the vigilance of an over-zealous cartographer.

'That is so.' Sober, factual. That was how I should respond.

'Did Agnes know about this relationship?'

To let her see that this was not easy to talk about, I glanced at my feet and studied the tips of my shoes for three seconds. Then I lifted my head and looked at her, hoping she realised that I responded at some cost – *it was hellishly painful* - but that nevertheless, despite that, I was making an effort to do my utmost to be frank and open.

'No.'

'Agnes has left you, hasn't she?'

'Yes.'

'What was her reason for leaving you?'

'She found out about it. My relationship with Katinka.'

'But didn't you just say that she didn't know about it?'

'Yes, but not before. She knew nothing about it before Katinka was murdered.'

'Well now, Joe, let's take things in order. Your lover is found murdered, and then your wife discovers that you have been having an affair with the deceased.'

'Yes.'

'How did Agnes find out that you and Katinka had had an affair?'

'I told her.'

'Why?'

'Because she asked me. She sensed that something was wrong.'

Thea turned her head and adopted a *sympathetic* expression. 'That must have been difficult.'

'It was fucking hellish.'

'Fucking hellish,' she repeated. 'Can you explain what you mean by that?'

I looked at her. A slip. *Fucking.* I shouldn't have used that word. She was looking for aggressive, unbalanced tendencies in the person being interviewed. Me. A motive, a reason for hating Katinka. But wouldn't it be even more suspicious if I showed no reaction at all, and instead sat unmoved, answering her questions with a robotic voice? *That* would have been even worse, I decided. I felt my face stiffen. I opened and shut my mouth, but couldn't say anything at all.

'Joe?'

I heard a man and a woman speaking in the passage outside. Their voices were clear for a moment as they passed the door, and then they were gone. I leaned back in the chair.

'Katinka and Agnes had been best friends,' Thea went on.

I nodded.

'It must have been a very stressful situation for you, having an intimate relationship with both of them?'

I didn't reply.

'Were you planning to leave Agnes?'

'No.'

'So why did you start a relationship with another woman?'

My eyes started wandering back and forth across her desk.

'I don't know.'

'You must have thought about why you did it.'

'Yes, I've thought about it, but …'

'But what?'

'I don't know what to say,' I mumbled, feeling ashamed of myself. 'I was tempted.'

'Tempted? And then you couldn't control yourself?'

It didn't sound very good when she put it that way.

'Well, no. I wouldn't have said it like that.'

167

'How would you have said it, then?'

'I felt dead,' I replied quickly. Be sober and objective, I thought to myself, don't answer so fast. 'Remember that,' I said out loud.

'What?'

'Nothing.'

She looked at me with surprise.

'She phoned you just before midnight on the night she was killed. Have you any idea why?'

'No. She had been helping me …,' I stammered, 'with the book. Perhaps there was something she … wanted to say …'

'Katinka had already found a new lover. Had that something to do with it?'

Thea appeared sly and cunning. Had she convinced herself that she had 'found something on me'?

'Did you know that Katinka had started an affair with another man?'

I coughed, to clear a little phlegm from deep in my throat. 'Excuse me.'

'Are you alright?'

'I had something in my throat.'

'That's OK. How did you react to Katinka having found another man?'

I wanted to say 'That doesn't make sense,' but managed to say 'Where did you hear that from?'

'Didn't you know?'

I shook my head. 'It's not surprising.'

'Not surprising?' Thea leaned over the desk.

'She was your childhood sweetheart, wasn't she?' Hadn't you gone on being in love with her for over twenty years? Hadn't you taken a lot of risks to be with her? Why then was it not surprising that she found someone else?'

I cleared my throat again. To say nothing would appear suspicious. I would look like a guilty party, considering how he could manage to present himself as the opposite of what he really is. The way you are sitting and thinking here, I thought to myself, is just the way a suspect would behave. He would consider and weigh each word carefully because he doesn't entirely trust himself.

What was it Montaigne wrote? Every movement reveals us. We reveal ourselves with everything we do, with the way we speak and the way we hold our tongue. We try to conceal ourselves, but our efforts make us even more visible.

'Did she say anything when she called?'

'I couldn't get hold of my phone. When I rang back, hers was switched off and all I got was an answering machine.'

'Are you sure you didn't talk with her that evening?'

'Yes.'

Thea doesn't like me. She doesn't want to show that when she's with Jenny, but as soon as Jenny leaves the room, she reverts to her artificially friendly façade.

'We have technicians checking through all her conversations and text messages,' Thea continued. 'If you feel there is anything you ought to tell me, now may be the time.'

A fan started humming in the adjacent office. I looked at the thin walls. How did they manage to work in such conditions? Thea leaned back a little and turned a ballpoint pen between her fingers.

'Where were you between nine and eleven o'clock the Friday evening Katinka was murdered?'

'At home.'

'Think about it.'

'What?'

'What did you do after you had been at home?'

I looked at her lowered eyebrows and the fine lines at the corners of her eyes. I couldn't lie. She knew I wasn't at home all that evening.

I coughed. 'I was out running.'

'Yes, go on.'

I coughed again.

169

'Describe your jogging route.'

I shut my eyes. My head felt like lead. The leg of the chair creaked, and for a moment I imagined it collapsing under the weight of my head.

'My jogging route?'

'Yes. Describe it to me.'

'You know where it goes.'

'Explain it to me.'

'OK. From Sandermosen Station I run up the hill towards Sinober.'

'And on the way?'

'On the way I pass the Moen family's hut.'

'That evening, Joe, did you notice anything in particular? Did you meet anyone up there?'

I saw the old wooden hut between the branches. 'No.'

'Nothing unusual?'

'No.'

'When you came to the Moen family's hut … look at me, Joe.'

I looked up. 'Yes?'

'Did you see a light in the window?' Her voice stung my ears. 'Did you stop and walk along the path to the hut? Did you see her in the window? Did you go up to the door and into the hut? What was she wearing? Do you remember what happened? Were you excited? Did you argue?'

I saw Katinka's face in the window. There was something very sad about it now, as if she knew that she was about to die.

'Have you …' The tears were welling up. '… found …' Anger and despair surged through my head. I leaned over the edge of her desk but couldn't remember standing up from the chair. It was as if a piece had been edited out of the conversation. I looked round in confusion and grasped Thea's cold little hand. The tears were now running down my cheeks. '… forensic evidence?'

'Please sit down, Joe.'

I sank back down into the chair and dried my tears. My head felt unbearably heavy again.

'You may think you're smart,' she said quietly, 'but do you think you can fool me with your crocodile tears?'

'What?'

'You can't be trusted, Joe. You're hiding something.'

I was halfway up from the chair before I managed to compose myself.

Behave normally. Calmly, rationally, innocently. I sat down again and tried to smile. 'I'm sorry. I'm an author,' I said, as calmly as I could. 'I'm too nervous to be a criminal. I could never, never have been able to kill anybody.'

Her lips curled in a sneer. 'If someone tells me that they would never, never have committed a crime, I immediately think there's something wrong.

'Sometimes people do just say what they think.'

'In criminal cases, honesty is not the human quality which carries most weight.'

'Do you think I'm lying?'

'I don't know.'

'I'm just a little nervous.'

She fingered the ballpoint pen again, taking the top off and on and putting the pen down again. 'The guilty are generally more nervous than the innocent.'

'Nobody is really fully innocent.'

'So what are you guilty of?'

'Unfaithfulness.'

'Is that all?'

'That's bad enough.'

'So why can't I stop thinking that there's something wrong?'

I shut my eyes again, totally exhausted. My voice seemed to come from far away. 'Do you really think I killed her?'

'Why do you shut your eyes?'

171

I opened them. 'Don't you think it would be strange?' I said quickly.

'What would be strange?'

'If I stuffed a page from my own book into the mouth of the woman I had killed?'

'How do you know about the page from the book?'

I didn't want to say anything about that. I didn't know whether Jenny had told Thea that she had let me see the page, or whether she had shown it to me 'under the table' to help me by giving me a hint that I was going to be dragged into the case whether I wanted to or not, quite irrespective of whether I had anything to do with it.

'I don't understand how you are thinking,' Thea continued.

'No.'

'Perhaps you just want us to find out.'

'Why should I want that?'

'Maybe you want to be caught.'

'Do you really believe that nonsense?'

She had no intention of answering, but if she didn't believe what she had said, why had she said it? She didn't trust what I was saying. If she really believed that I was a ruthless killer, she would have frightened me out of my skin.

She nodded slowly now, as if she had heard what I was thinking.

'You were out running that evening, at around the time Katinka was killed. You could have stopped at the hut, killed Katinka, put her in the chest and been back at Frysja by eleven o'clock.'

I tried to imagine myself putting Katinka into the chest, shutting it and dragging it into the woods. I must brace myself, be a man, think logically. More logically than her. 'Does that make sense to you?'

'Does what make sense?'

'That I would kill Katinka just because she was with somebody else?'

172

She looked at the ballpoint pen as if it was a source of enormously interesting information. 'I don't think anything makes sense.'

'Can I ask you about something now?'

She nodded briefly.

'Have you discovered anything more about George Nymann?'

She put the pen down.

'No. We've found no trace of George Nymann in Norway. He has no registered address here, and no registered telephone number. Nothing.'

'What about the Irish prison? Have you checked that?'

'He served a sentence in Ireland, but there's no trace of him after his release. There's no evidence that he actually is here in Oslo. He seems to have vanished.'

I felt a pang in my head and thought about Emma and our swimming trip to Stilla. 'We saw him at Stilla, Emma and I. Several others must have seen him that day.'

'I've spoken to Emma on the phone,' said Thea without a shred of sympathy or compassion, 'but she told me that she didn't know who George was and that she had never met an unknown man at Stilla.'

A network of threads was closing in on me. I put my hand into my pocket and took out my cellphone. I wanted to call Agnes, talk to Emma, get her to tell Thea what had really happened. I keyed Agnes's number and held the phone tightly. I had asked Emma not to talk about George to anybody, because I hadn't wanted Agnes to know. Emma now believed that the police shouldn't get to know about it either.

'Who are you phoning?'

'Agnes.'

No connection.

'Nobody answering?'

'The network coverage isn't so good down there. She's at her father's hut in Stavern. Emma's there too. I just wanted to call her to get her to …'

'Change her statement?'

I put the phone down. 'You don't understand. She'll explain exactly what happened.'

'You mean: exactly what you want her to tell me.'

I shook my head. I didn't have the strength to quibble any more. Thea would just win. I gave up. How long was it since I had slept properly? Far too long. My thoughts were blurred. I needed to rest.

I could picture them, Agnes and Emma, in the hammock strung between the plum trees in the garden below the hut. It was swinging slowly back and forth under the canopy of leaves. From down by the shore I heard the sound of the dinghy swinging at its moorings. I walked over the dewy, damp grass down towards the pier.

'Joe?'

I heard a drawer being opened.

'I need to show you this.' Thea took something out of the drawer and placed his manuscript on the table in front of me. 'This autobiographical manuscript of yours gives me a lot to think about, both regarding Katinka's murder and about your attempt to drag this George Nymann into the case.'

I couldn't take my eyes off the document. She had said 'this manuscript of yours,' but all I asked was where she had got it from.

'That isn't important, but what is important is to be clear about whether what appears in the manuscript relates to what happened in reality.'

'What?'

'Whether you have done what is written here ...'

I pushed the dinghy off from the pier and started rowing out into the bay. The house and the garden back on land grew smaller and smaller, and then I lost sight of the plum tree and the hammock and their heads. The dinghy floated faster and faster away from land. The wind caught the boat. I was out on the open sea, gazing around.

Thea's voice: 'Your editor says she has received a similar manuscript. She tells me that the style is remarkably like yours.'

'My style?' I mumbled, though I think my voice was inaudible. 'I didn't write that.'

'Can you prove it?'

'Prove it?'

'There's a lot to suggest that you are the author.' She poked at the manuscript with a finger.

'Is there? So what?'

'I can't go into that, Joe. I'll call you in for an interview.'

'Can I go home now?' My tongue felt like a lead weight in my mouth.

She nodded.

'Go home and get some sleep, but don't go out of town.'

In the lift down to reception I caught sight of a deathly pale face with swollen eyes. I rested my forehead against the cool glass.

23

The kitchen window was a thin shield, protecting me from oppressive darkness. I knew I ought to sleep, but I couldn't. Instead I switched on the radio and brewed a big pot of coffee. The late news presenter spoke in a drowsy voice about climate research and Arctic ice melt. I couldn't follow so switched the radio off, poured coffee into a mug and added sugar.

Opening George's manuscript again I immediately understood that the purpose of the text was to destroy the author. He wanted to murder the author's reputation, crush his integrity and render him an outcast.

All that was on the cover page was the Italic letter U. The first line was: 'My name is Joe Uddermann. I am an author. I killed somebody.'

I read that several times, but could go no further and pushed the manuscript aside. 'My name is Joe …' Was he asking a paradoxical question? Was it possible to be both a constructive author and a destructive murderer?

I read the three sentences again. That was not the main point. He was presenting himself as me. I was the one who had killed somebody. I read on, one sentence at a time. Pause. Another sentence. Another sentence. After a short introduction, the text described Joe's sexual jealousy as an adult:

'I couldn't sleep. My perverted lust was sickening me. Even though our relationship had ended, my thoughts churned

around Katinka. I saw her hands.
I put my face against her feet and

I blushed, drank more coffee and

'I would do anything at all to g
enjoy being with her. I was alw
me. My fear that it would come
    'I looked at her with a servile
own behaviour. I was a dog, eating
dogs. When she kicked me aside I came back to
kicking. I couldn't get enough of it. Without her, I was
nothing. I loved her scorn. I loved it when she kicked me. I
would crawl for her. I licked her feet. I wanted her to kick
me in the face and call me a cur. I hid whimpering under the
table. She couldn't bear me any more.
'I was more dog than human.'

I read a little more:

'For several weeks, I could think only of her. I hoped that she
would take me back and we could start afresh. I was willing
to give up everything; my writing, my family, the house were
of little consequence compared to her. I had been happy for
a few short months. Now everything was ruined. I couldn't
stop thinking about it. I didn't sleep for days, didn't eat. Then
one day came her message.
    '*We can't meet any more.*
    '"Why can't we meet?"
    'No answer. It felt as if I had been diagnosed with a
dangerous, contagious disease.
    '"Why don't you answer?"
    'No answer.
    '"I want to see you."
    'No answer.

177

ee your face."

r.

ndreds of messages on her cellphone, but she never
ck. It was like shouting down a well. All I heard was
o of my own despairing voice.

ventually I wrote her a last message:
'This can't go on.

'No. It was unacceptable.

'How in Hell could I get her to realise that she had made a serious mistake?

'Days and weeks passed. I was getting thinner by the day. I started having dark thoughts. She had said that she didn't want to see me any more, and I began to understand that my fear of losing her had driven her as far away from me as it was possible to be. She didn't love me, she scorned me. She didn't want to see me.

'She was a whore, a monstrous cunt.'

My style? Was that really *my style*?

'I can see you.
'I never lose sight of you.
'I watch you leave the house in the morning.
'I watch you drive along Frysjaveien.
'I know where you work.
'I know nearly everything about you.
'One of us has to go.'

Reading through George's forged manuscript with its sentences resembling mine, I thought what a fraudster he was. Not only was he not admitting authorship, he was also stealing my identity. The confusion was dragging me down into this muddy text.

You must read carefully, I muttered to myself. Simply, word for word, as if you have just learned to read.

178

I turned to the end of the manuscript and read the last section:

'Hell is a place in your head. When a boy is locked in a cellar, for example, he can create a whole world of misery in the few minutes he is shut in there. When the trapdoor is opened and he realises that he is not going to die there after all, he still sees everything from the perspective of the cellar, as if a pair of black contact lenses have been placed over his eyes.

'It takes time, let me tell you, to get rid of these lenses. Some people never manage, because they have become convinced that the world really looks like that. Others live in a dream world.

'I stand in front of the mirror, studying my face to look for the monstrous features which characterise me as a murderer, but it just looks odd. I don't think I'm nearly ugly enough.

'I'm still innocent in other people's eyes, but all will become clear when you read this.

'Isn't it legitimate to perform the long and careful task of writing an antidote to correct a falsehood? Doesn't sitting month after month at the writing desk require sincerity? And is it not therefore irrefutable that the text is truthful? Otherwise it could not be written. I'm convinced of that.

'Now I'll tell you how things turned out for the man who got the blame for my crimes. That is who this book will be about, for he is the really interesting one. I was a scoundrel and a coward, but he was an enormously interesting person.'

That was the last sentence in the uncompleted manuscript, which apparently was to be continued in one way or another. I stared at the sentence, read it several times and began to scream.

24

In the morning I found a broken roof tile on the grass among the apple trees. I fetched the ladder and climbed onto the roof. There had been unusually heavy snowfall through the winter which I hadn't been diligent in clearing away. Several tiles were broken and would need to be replaced, and there were ominous cracks in the roofing fabric.

I removed the most damaged and checked there was nothing loose, then sat in the garden with a glass of wine and looked up. The whole house was crooked, but I hadn't noticed that the middle of the roof sagged so much. I went into the house to call the builder and ask him to take a look. It shouldn't be like that. While I was speaking to him I thought about Swedenborg's description of Hell, a short story I had pondered many times.

A learned scholar inherits a palace; this is roughly how Swedenborg's story begins. He is happy, because now he has the opportunity to complete his life's work, an encyclopaedic project of great significance. In the library he works in deep concentration while, little by little, the prosperity of the palace disappears. Little things go first. One morning the friendly old servant vanishes, followed by the other servants, one by one, until nobody is left. The tableware and the delicious meals which were served morning and evening disappear. The clocks stop, and the books and shelves depart from the library. The floors begin to crumble under his feet, the walls crack and the windows fall out.

He had felt sure that he was secure. Free of worries he had

nothing to do but concentrate on his writing. Now there is nothing left. He is living in a crumbling ruin of rubbish and dust until, one morning the roof goes, and he stands alone in a desert. When he looks at the sand dunes and at his cracked hands and ragged clothes, he realises that he has been dead all this time, that the palace was a hallucination, a vision, and that he has arrived in Hell.

I looked suspiciously around the crooked house which my father had bought and renovated. The roof had shifted, there were fine cracks in the walls and little ants marched across the floor. The builder would be coming next week, but then a thought struck me: What if I'm not here next week?

Where would I be then? In prison. In custody.

Feeling sick, I went out to the toilet. The floor felt cold beneath my kneecaps and I retched several times, but all I could bring up was a little lukewarm fluid. I showered in warm water and tried to dismiss the picture which came up whenever I closed my eyes, of George opening the door from the garden and walking into the living room, black water dripping from his fingertips.

Lying on the sofa I rang Agnes's number repeatedly, just to hear her voice saying: 'Leave a message and I'll call you back.'

My phone ringing wakened me. Fiddling with the answering button, I rolled off the sofa and banged my elbow as I fell to the floor. It was Agnes.

'Joe?'

'Agnes? Where are you? Are you OK?'

'Yes, we're fine. Didn't Dad tell you that?'

'Yes, but ... I was so worried ...'

'What about?'

'That something might have happened to you.'

'I'm sorry,' she said quietly. 'I should have called.'

'I've been at your Dad's house. What's happened? A break-in?'

181

The phone was quiet for a few seconds, except for a rustling sound.

'Agnes?'

'I'm here,' she whispered.

'The neighbour said there had been a break-in.'

'Yes.'

'But nothing was taken.'

'No.' Her voice was barely audible. I got up from the floor and pressed the cellphone hard against my ear. I wanted to hear the sound of her breath. 'Emma was scared,' she said, 'and I was beginning to feel brittle. So we drove down to Stavern.'

'OK.' Worrying silence. 'Agnes?' Silence, silence. 'Are you there?'

'Jenny has been to see me,' she said.

'Jenny? What on earth did she want?' I realised that I sounded aggressive.

'She wanted to talk about you, Joe.'

'About me? What did that traitor say about me, then?'

'Please, Joe.'

'What?'

'You're upset, Joe.'

'Yes, when you just disappear suddenly, of course I'm upset. So long as the two of you are OK, I'm fine. I was beginning to think all sorts of strange things.'

'She was worried about you. She said that you had been at the hut and that things didn't look good, but she wouldn't answer when I asked what she meant by that.'

'By what?'

'That it didn't look good that you were loitering in the woods around the hut.'

'Was that what she said?'

'Something like that.'

'Is there something you haven't told me, Agnes?' I held the phone away from my ear for a few seconds. Agnes wasn't

182

answering. '*Something like that*? What did she say, exactly?'

'I don't remember. Not exactly.'

'Oh well. I was wondering if we could take a trip to the amusement park at Tusenfryd one day,' I said, as calmly as I could.

'Tusenfryd?'

'Yes, with Emma.'

'We'll need to talk about that another time, Joe.'

'Have you come back to town?'

'Yes.'

'It was a very short visit to Stavern?'

She coughed.

'Can I speak to Emma?'

'She's sleeping.'

'OK. Do you remember that time we went walking in the mountains?'

'What?'

'The time when ...' I glanced at two little ants crawling one after the other across the parquet flooring ... 'when Emma was conceived.'

'For God's sake, Joe.'

'It was such a good time,' I said without pausing to reflect. 'I mean, not just the conception, no, that wasn't what I meant though that was good too. No, I meant the whole trip, where there were just the two of us and we were in love, do you remember that, and everything was fine and I don't think I've ever been so happy as I was then, together with you, you were so wonderful.'

'Joe ...'

'I remember that we sat on the steps outside the hut and I leaned my head on your shoulder and thought that we were glued together, like Siamese twins, and that was slightly scary but most of all I was happy and felt that life had meaning, and that I could happily go on just like that, without changes, just exactly that and nothing else. Do you know what I mean?

I'm really very sorry that I've hurt you and I understand that you're angry. You've obviously every right to be angry but, remember this, just that ... that ... I love you.'

There was a pause.

'I understand,' she said quietly.

'I promise ...,' I started, but my voice broke. 'I don't think I should say anything more.'

'Maybe not.'

But I wanted to say it again, that I loved her, really loved her, really really loved her, perhaps she hadn't heard me the first time, I'd spoken so quietly, but I ought to have shouted it into the telephone, couldn't say it soon enough and loud enough and often enough, and what's more I also wanted to say that I'd been thinking about it for a long time and that I had never in my life been more sure of anything.

'You sound exhausted, Joe.'

I swallowed and cleared my throat. 'Do I?'

'Yes.'

'I was just on my way to bed.'

'That sounds like a good idea.'

'I'm glad,' I said.

'What about?'

'That you – that both of you – have come back to town.'

'Everything's fine.'

'Remember to lock all the doors.'

'I've done that.'

'Good. Would you like me to come over? I mean, I can just sit in the car and keep an eye on the house, in case someone comes.'

'There's no need for that. I've spoken to the police.'

'Alright, I'll stay here. Be careful.'

'Yes.' I held the phone close to my ear to hear her lovely voice. 'Sleep well, Joe.'

'Yes. You too.'

She rang off. I sat on the sofa and listened to the dialling tone for a few seconds. My heart was thumping. What was it she had said? That I seemed tired. It was the first time in ages that she had cared about how I was.

I lay down on the sofa again and shut my eyes. I saw Jenny's face right in front of my eyes, as if she was there in the room. She bent closer and closer, right down to my face.

You're not yourself.

I gave a start. A glass fell to the floor and smashed. Good God, I was a wreck, a nervous ruin of the man I had been a few days before. Picking the fragments up from the floor I thought how George had been messing about in my head. Everything in my head had been moved, nothing was where it should be, though some bits were recognisable.

What he had written was pure lie, but there was some truth in it too. The feelings I had for Katinka ... the thoughts which churned round and round and the confusion and the feeling of being put down ... wasn't some of that *amazingly accurate*?

In the bathroom I splashed cold water on my face. I was breathing heavily, and I felt a stabbing pain in my chest. Was I going to have a heart attack? I didn't dare look at my face in the mirror. A silverfish bug scurried across the bathroom floor and disappeared down a crack.

I clench my eyelids hard again. Everything suggests that I have come to a dead end. I don't know who I am, and don't know why I'm alive.

Everything I see seems so artificial and contrived. The world is a fragile stage set and all the men and women merely ham actors. Their lines are like parodies because they don't take the trouble to rehearse precise movement and lifelike mimicry.

The feeling of seeing through them is convincing, but I don't know what lies behind. Only that everything is an illusion and that life is but a play of shadows. How could somebody who knows so little manage to write meaningfully about anything at all? Can I carry on as an author, with so amazingly little knowledge?

I open my eyes. Can't go on thinking like this.

Back in the living room I lay down on the floor and tried to think clearly, as an investigator would.

What was I looking for? The motivation! Everything starts with that. What did he want to do? To blacken me, take revenge for what I had written. He wanted to ruin my authority (if I had any) and my credibility (not so difficult). Even if the reader didn't believe it was me who had written George's text, it would still cast a doubtful shadow over everything and would inevitably paint a picture of me as suspect and unreliable and contemptible.

He wouldn't give up until he had rubbed my face in the dirt.

I got up and paced back and forth between the rooms, from the kitchen to the living room and back to the kitchen where I leaned over the bench. Half a cup of cold coffee. A half eaten slice of bread on a plate. A dry, shrivelled slice of ham. Sooner or later the police would discover that the text had not been written by me, but perhaps that didn't matter any more. This was just the first stage, I thought, on the way to his finale.

'You'll need to get hold of his motivation to find out what he's planning,' I mumbled, but that just sounded like an abstract hypothesis.

What was the next concrete step? To have me condemned? I felt naked.

I walked out onto the road, stood barefoot on the asphalt and looked into the dark with what almost felt like pleasure. Peering towards the river I saw nothing but mist and darkness and, for a few seconds I believed: I am a normal man looking down towards the river in the dusk; everything is alright; my name is Joe; nobody is trying to kill me.

I stood smiling for a while, trying to enjoy the view. The

river was running so gently, the water gurgling peacefully below the mist. I would be happier if I relaxed like this all the time, I thought.

With a ghostly smile on my lips, I walked back into the house, locked myself in and stood in the dark in the living room. I felt calmer now. Frysjaveien, I thought. Why did you write about that?

I can see you, you wrote.

Was *that* what you wanted to show me?

I never lose sight of you.

I lowered myself into the armchair.

Vebjorn and Katinka lived in Frysjaveien. Were you telling me something unwittingly? Was that where you were staying, in one of the office blocks with a window overlooking Frysjaveien?

From the office building you could look down on the shabby terraced house that Vebjorn and Katinka had moved into, and the overgrown garden full of weeds, with a rusty, lop-sided clothes airer. The lilac hedge round their property shielded them from all sides, but not from above. From your window, you were watching them through binoculars. Double doors opened onto the garden. Vebjorn was sitting in the shade of a sun-flecked parasol with his cellphone and a bottle of beer.

Under the brim of his dirty straw hat did you catch a glimpse of the peevish look in his eyes? There had been something wretched and cowardly about Vebjorn. That was how we remembered him. As he grew older he did all he could to appear hard, but inside was he not still a coward?

Did you look through the terrace door, right into the bedroom? She stood at the foot of the bed, undressed and lay down. You adjusted the focus on the binoculars and looked through the window at her naked toes, ankles, thighs and the hand covering her private parts.

Stop. Go back. Out of bed, out of the bedroom, out of

Vebjorn and Katinka's house, back, even further back. There, at a window, with the binoculars held to your eyes. You want me to think about her and not about you, but I want to think about you, and I see you with my mind's eye.

You press the binoculars hard against your eyes, so hard it's painful.

The bathing place where you met me is only a few hundred metres from your window. You could have sat there looking down at Emma bathing that morning. You saw her playing with her dolls. You saw me sleeping. You hurried down.

You walked along the path, right down to the weir. From there you could look without anybody noticing you. Did you lure Emma over to the other side of the river? Did you signal to her in secret while I was asleep? Had you hidden a doll between the stones?

How did you get her to trust you?

Did you make yourself helpful and mild and innocent?

Did you talk to her in that little whistling voice of yours?

Which building are you sitting in?

Which window are you looking out from?

Are you looking down at the road and the lamplights on the slope down towards Stilla? Are you scanning from lamppost to lamppost?

I opened my laptop and was soon into Google Maps, looking at all the old office buildings in Frysjaveien. Rectangular grey roofs of different sizes, rows of small and medium sized buildings along the straight line of Frysjaveien: Algeta Ltd., Mortensen Printing House, Nlogic, Progress Engineering Company, Noatabene Publishing, Keli Ltd.

Where are you?

Several of the office buildings were close to the corner of Frysjaveien and Kjelsasveien, and Vebjorn and Katinka's shabby terraced house. I scrutinised the aerial photo. In the

Mortensen Printing House building there was a separate section on the roof of the main building.

Have you rented a room there? In your own name? No! You would never rent something in your own name. You would have rented it in my name, so that it looked as if I was the one watching her.

You stood at the window in the office building, in the classic posture of a man holding a spyglass to his eyes as in the old Hitchcock film, *Rear Window*. That was how you stood, leaning crookedly across the windowsill.

At night you went down to the river. You were still being choked by something which was growing inside you like a malignant tumour. You lay down with your head on a stone and stared up at the clouds disappearing over the old sawmill.

You thought about Katinka and her hut in Maridalen. You lit a cigarette and lay smoking. You saw her sleeping face and imagined her opening her eyes and looking at you – she was silent for a few seconds – and then she started screaming.

Stop.

You're losing the plot.

Go back. Open your eyes.

The screen had gone blank. I pressed a key and it came to life again.

Google maps, the aerial photo of Frysjaveien.

I went on Yellow Pages and looked for my own name in the list of businesses. There I was: *Joe Uddermann, programme developer, 71 Frysjaveien, 5th floor.*

189

25

Heavy rain-clouds were scurrying across the Frysja sky. During the night the rain would surely beat against the windows and inundate the gardens until the muddy water overflowed onto the streets. I stood by the garden fence and looked up at the clouds being tossed back and forth and into each other by the fresh breeze.

Driving slowly along Frysjaveien I looked carefully at either side. When I opened the window, I could hear the roar of the Brekke falls and my fatigue vanished. I felt clear-headed and ready.

I called Jenny just before 4.00 am. She answered drowsily, 'Yes?'

'I'm sitting in the car outside an office building in Frysjaveien.'

'What the hell are you doing there in the middle of the night?'

'George Nymann has rented an office in the building just across from me. There's a light in the window, I think he's in there now.'

'He's rented an office?' She didn't sound convinced.

I gave her the address. 'It's in my name.'

'In your name?'

'Yes, he's rented an office in my name. Programme developer, that's what he calls himself – or me.'

She hesitated, but then said: 'Stay where you are, Joe. I'll be there in fifteen minutes.'

I dropped the phone on the passenger seat and looked

190

across at the entrance to the building. The street number was written in big letters on a placard above the dirty glass door. On the fifth floor a light was on where 'Joe Uddermann' had his office. Was that somebody standing in the window? Was that his shape, little more than a shadow, sliding out of sight when he saw my car?

The pulse in my neck throbbed. Now I didn't know: was it I who was looking at him or he who was looking at me? I had convinced myself that I was in control, that I was directing events, but maybe that was what he wanted me to believe so that I could be more easily manipulated into a corner.

My brain felt as if it was shrinking in my skull and I imagined I could smell him beside me: resin, metal and burnt rubber. I leaned out and vomited on the road. My eyes were watering. 'You forgot to eat,' I mumbled as I clambered in again

In the glove compartment I found a half-eaten chocolate wafer only three or four days old, and only then realised how hungry I was.

I looked up at the fifth floor again. The light was still on, but there were no shapes in the window. My cellphone rang and I answered without looking at the display. Emma's voice was barely audible: *'Daddy?'*

The dashboard clock said 04.13. 'Emma? Are you awake at this time? Where are you, dear?'

'I don't know.'

The phone pressed right into my ear. 'You don't know?'

'No.' The voice vanished.

I should have driven up to their place instead. I should have hidden in the garden to keep an eye on the house. 'Emma?'

There was a crackling on the line. *'He drove me out here.'*

'Out where?'

The light was still on in the window. I had been so sure he was in there.

191

'*To a house,*' she gasped anxiously.

'Emma, where's Mummy?'

A lorry approached at the end of Frysjaveien. The front was red and the windows in the driver's cabin were tinted.

'*I don't know. I was asleep, and then I wakened up here.*'

'OK, OK, What does it look like, where you are?'

'*It's an old hut.*'

A hut.

'*And a shed.*'

A shed.

Her voice disappeared. Buzzing. The lorry drove slowly by.

'Emma?'

A tearing sound, as of paper being ripped into pieces.

'*This is his phone.*'

'Where is he?'

'*I always remember it, Daddy.*'

'What's that, my dear?'

'*Your number.*'

'Well done. That's good, Emma. Tell me, where's George?'

Then we lost the connection.

I followed the lorry along Frysjaveien and continued out along Maridalsveien, past the fields and the river, as fast as I could. The spruce forest closed in on either side, the treetops reaching up towards the tumbling clouds. Why didn't it start to rain? I thought how I could strangle him and pictured what he would look like when he was dead, with his lips silent and his eyes and hands motionless. The fields beside the road looked like the backs of sleeping giants.

The car skidded on a bend.

It's a trap, I thought. He's enticing me out there, but when I arrive there's nobody there. I call her name, but there's nobody there. The door of the hut is open. I go in, shove the rug aside and open the trap door and scrabble around in

192

the dark. Beside an old hammer there is a little pink lump of something, like a scallop. I pick it up and feel the damp flesh, and then I see that it's a tongue.

Stop.

The gravel road towards Sandermosen is narrow and visibility is poor. I'm driving too fast and the wheels are churning up clouds of black dust, but I can't slow down.

I key Jenny's number while I'm driving, and explain where I'm going.

26

A solitary van was parked at Sandermosen Station. I scrambled out of the car and looked around. A robin was singing. The wind had scattered the clouds, and the area was bathed in blue early morning light. One of the windows in the old building was broken and the information boards were hanging askew, and the old party bus was still there.

I stepped over the tracks and walked into the woods. Bright threads of light shone down through the spruce trees and around my feet as I stumbled along the stony path to the clearing and the hut. The door was open.

There was a light in the kitchen window. Was somebody in there? Sweat ran into my eyes as I strained to look. I dried my face with my shirt and whispered Emma's name. Daylight was growing stronger.

My shoes sank into the wet grass as I stepped over the remains of the police cordon. I shouted her name and, in that same instant, saw her sitting on a tree stump with the cellphone in her hands. I went over to her.

'Hello, my love.'

She looked as if she was asleep, and I immediately recognised that she had been doped and couldn't move.

'Emma?'

I laid my hand on her head and she leaned head back with a faraway look in her eyes. Her shoulder was cold under her thin nightdress.

'Hello, my love.' I stroked her hair away from her eyes. Shock, I thought. 'Are you cold?'

She shook her head.

'What are you doing here?' I asked.

She looked at me in surprise, and then looked away. I followed her gaze across the clearing, towards the tree.

Through the branches, above the roof of the hut, I saw his gumboots. He had stuffed his trouser legs into them, which was why they hadn't fallen off. Early morning sunlight filtered through the leaves of the trees, and the darkness and dew were dispersing. Now I could see his body and his head and the rope round his neck, tied with a slipknot to the thickest branch. He had bitten his lip, and his jaw was covered with blood and saliva. His tongue was hanging out and his face was stiff and distorted. He already looked as if he had been dead for many weeks.

Emma was breathing deeply, as if she had been holding her breath for a long time. She had shut her eyes and sat in suspended animation, just breathing, and I realised that the corpse hanging from the tree was the end of one story but just the beginning of another, less dramatic but just as painful.

I picked her up and put my hand over her eyes. I didn't want her to see it, but of course it was too late. She had been watching him swing for ages. 'Try to forget about it,' I whispered, cuddling her close.

She didn't answer, but went on breathing deeply and regularly, as if she was asleep. The sun began to appear above the treetops.

Walking down the hillside with my little daughter in my arms, I thought: This is what he planned so carefully, that I would stand on this accursed ground with Emma in my arms, struggling to find words and helplessly and inadequately stroking her head. *That* was the plot which gave him strength to climb the tree, tie the knot round his neck and jump from the branch.

That had been his aim all the time: to plant a disturbing,

destructive disharmony in our brains, to know that his personality would grow bigger long after he was gone.

Jenny met us at the parking place and took Emma carefully into her car, saying that she should just sit there for a little while and she would take her home to Agnes.

For a few minutes, Jenny and I stood alone in the parking place while I tried to explain what had happened. I don't remember much of what I said, but I remember how she stroked my cheek like she used to do. 'I always knew you were innocent,' she said.

Then we heard the sirens.

Epilogue, 2013

During my first days in the hospital I became convinced that the rooms and the corridors were shrinking. With every day that passed they seemed to become a few square centimetres smaller and the air became thicker. Nevertheless, the hospital was where I wanted to be. I knew I wasn't well.

I certainly couldn't be in the house in Frysja where the feeling of claustrophobia was unbearable and I had begun to suspect the neighbours of bugging the place. Their intention, I thought, was to dig up information to assemble into a coherent accusation of a crime which I hadn't committed and so remove such a bringer of bad fortune from their neighbourhood.

It was there that I had shut myself in the basement, and where I had the fatal and insane idea of writing a novel about myself and my thoughts. It would have no plot, and no fictional characters. The text would consist only of the unedited results of my captured thoughts. This would not be the first time an author had tried to do such a thing, but this text was to be more radical than anything before. Its title was to be: *Author Joe Uddermann's Absolutely Uncensored Basement Thoughts*. The title in itself showed what a bad state I was in with paranoia, claustrophobia and delusions of grandeur.

In the hospital, at least there were other people: nurses, psychologists, cleaners and other patients. Mostly I spoke with the psychologists, being cautious about the others. Although I didn't have anything against them, I wasn't one hundred per cent confident that they wished me well. What's more, I wasn't like them, the overweight women with chronic depression or the skinny psychotics or the sly heroin addicts. In my case admission to hospital was the consequence of a temporary breakdown. After a few weeks everything would seem like a bad dream and I would be home again. So I told myself.

I wasn't in a locked ward, but it still felt like a prison cell and at night I couldn't stop thinking about the chest with Katinka's body inside. In the manuscript, George had described me as a murderer. If I was co-responsible for Katinka's death, wasn't it logical that the hospital room slowly metamorphosed into a cell? I felt I had been caught in a spiral I couldn't escape. When I wakened in the mornings, I lay for a while with my eyes shut, thinking: You have caused somebody's death and you are serving a just punishment.

The psychologists thought that writing would be good for me as writing can have a therapeutic, healing effect, provided my project wasn't 'too ambitious'. Not surprising, considering that most psychologists and therapists are storytellers first and foremost. So I sat at the table to write. I had given up the idiotic, childish idea of writing a text which captured my completely uncensored thoughts. Instead, I tried to write about what had happened after Katinka was murdered.

At the start I was fully decided that it shouldn't be 'too ambitious', but after only a few days I was again fully absorbed and very quickly began to doubt whether the exertions really were therapeutic. I wrote for whole days and on into the nights, putting enormous energy into the work, leaving my room only to eat and for the shortest possible conversation with one of the psychologists. I reassured them that my writing was proceeding at a calm, steady tempo with no danger of overexertion.

Then one morning a strange thing happened. I wakened at about half past five, immediately went to the little table in front of the window but didn't recognise the text. I couldn't believe I had written it. I was so amazed that I threw the pages into the waste paper basket.

I sat down and wrote the section afresh, about meeting George Nymann on the bridge at Stilla, trying to describe my feelings of anxiety and unreality, of being a witness to what had happened but not being able to control or direct my life. I tried to describe the confusion growing within me. When I sat at the table the following morning the same thing happened. What I had written seemed foreign and borrowed.

I wakened in the middle of the night, thinking that somebody else must have written my text. Somebody had sneaked in during the night, sat at the desk and rearranged what I had been working on all day and evening. I tried to sleep with one eye open ...

Writing was itself turning into a prison.

When the psychologist again asked how my work was going, I mumbled something about looking for something more real, something less *written*. When she looked at me with a mixture of surprise and anxiety I understood that I would need to correct the bad impression I was making. They mustn't think that the project was out of control and start imposing limits.

Now followed hour after hour of pondering, during which the literary flow dried up. I couldn't write because of the enormous ongoing task of thinking. The language of autobiography is a refuge for the author, but this refuge had become uncomfortable, uncanny and unrecognisable.

I no longer believed that writing about myself made the text more real. I was aiming for reality, but missing the target, and it dawned on me that the path to reality could not be followed impulsively, but only with unbounded patience.

The thought of abandoning the whole book was tempting, but every time I threw the manuscript into the bin I repented and pulled it out again. I thought: Write yourself out of the book. Perhaps *that* is the problem. *I* am getting in the way.

Who on earth should the book be about, then?

*

Towards the end of October I visited his grave in Grefsen churchyard. I hadn't been there since the funeral, and was struck by how big it was. The long rows of gravestones seemed strangely impressive. His grave was in the new section up by Old Kjelsas Street by a leaf-strewn path. For several minutes I stood looking at the stone with the simple inscription.

George Nymann
b. 1977 – d. 2012
Not forgotten

Who had taken the care to organise the inscription? I thought it could only have been George himself. There was something both hopeful and malicious about the two words.

I laid the book I had written on his gravestone.

The Consequences.

It was a novel about an author who goes to pieces.

I turned and walked quickly back to the house at Frysja where Agnes was due to bring Emma. It was my weekend to have her, and she couldn't wait alone for me. After what had happened she hated being alone.

I followed the footpath between the churchyard and the detached houses in Saturnveien. Everything seemed so peaceful, idyllic. A man was raking rotten leaves, concentrating on the work and wholly taken up in it. Although more at peace than for a long time, I wasn't entirely healthy yet. I still had deranged thoughts, but it could have been worse.

On the hillside behind Engebraten School, two fair-haired

boys were playing with scooters. The Aker River flowed dark and silent. A few ducks cackled noisily in alarm. Nothing can make silence scream.

I walked along the path towards my house. It was a calm autumn morning, but I couldn't stop thinking about the gravestone:

Not forgotten.